THE MOMENT

PETER HOLM JENSEN

THE MOMENT

PETER HOLM JENSEN

SPLICE

It is entirely conceivable that life's splendour forever lies in wait about each one of us in all its fullness, but veiled from view, deep down, invisible, far off. It is there, though, not hostile, not reluctant, not deaf. If you summon it by the right word, by its right name, it will come.

Kafka

MAP SHEWING
THE
LAND OF THE BROADS
&c. &c.

DRAWN BY E. R. SUFFLING
PUBLISHED BY
L. Upcott Gill, 170, Strand
LONDON W.C.

Scale of Miles

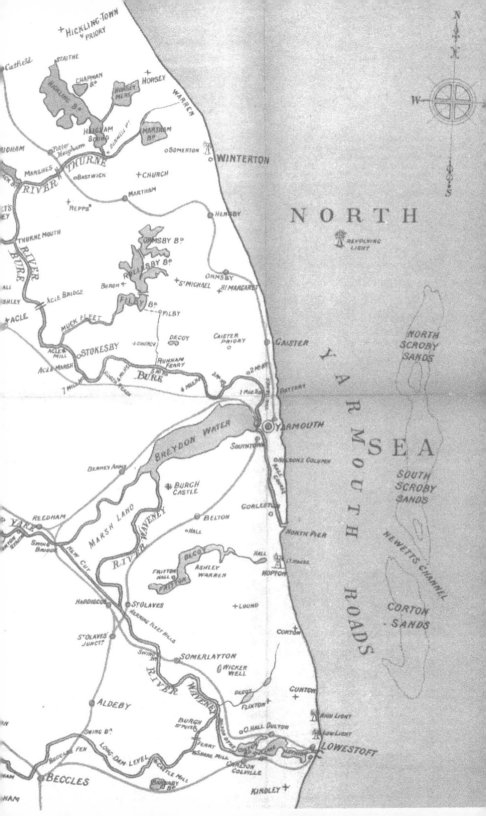

It's spring. S. seems to be settling in, though she sometimes misses the city. Today she asked T. to stop mowing the grass beside the dirt road that leads to his old farm so she could pick some wildflowers. He stopped, frowned, said she better do it quick. It was a joy to watch her move out there, snipping the stems with the kitchen scissors.

The other day she convinced T. not to kill the feral kittens born in his haybarn. She saw him on his way to the field with the kittens in a wooden box and a spade in his other hand. She ran to him and asked him to leave them until they'd been weaned. We'd take them in, she told him, keep one with us and give the rest away. He looked at her with his steady gaze. Senimenal girl, he said in that dry Norfolk tone. But she swayed him and he took the box back to the barn.

Sleepless at midnight. I've brought the laptop to the kitchen table, but I'm too tired to work. A mouse runs across the floor, stops and stares at me, twitches its nose and cocks an ear. I toy with the idea of opening a bottle but decide to go outside to smoke instead. A fox screeches under the moonlight. Or is it an owl? Does it matter?

Mistrust of writing, of words. Yet here I remain, laptop open, urged by something—what?—to write again after so long a silence. What do I want? The same as ever: to find words that can bring life closer, let it speak simply in me for once. But I start typing and watch lies roll across the screen. I'm in the way of myself. The words themselves, the ones I settle for, are in the way. In any case, didn't I come out here to get away from these kinds of questions?

After daybreak I brought S. tea and fruit in bed. We lay there awhile, chatting and laughing. Then, a day like most others: we worked, walked to the Co-op, returned to Rook Lane and worked some more until evening. Now she's making dinner.

In the evening we go to the Rose. Tricky to get there walking down the narrow road with cars roaring by. But worth it. The place is like a combination of all the good pubs I've been to. Mostly silence, broken only by some friendly local chatter. Clean wooden floors. No screens and no music, above all no music. We exchange some gossip with the landlord and I order my usual, the local farm cider: cool and crisp and dry. S. tries it for the first time. Go easy on this, I tell her, it's not to be trifled with. *You* go easy, she says softly, sipping her half. After a couple of pints I get stupid. Look at this, I say, holding up the glass to the light. The distillation of applehood. This is what Adam and Eve drank in Eden. One day, I say, I'll write a poem to this cider—an ode! An old boy at the bar turns to look at us. Can we go? S. asks sadly. I reluctantly agree.

I remember F., a real Norfolk old-timer. He was one of my drinking friends when I lived in Norwich and used to work in pubs on my laptop. He'd been a groundsman on a country estate before it was auctioned off to developers, luckily for him not before he could collect his pension. We'd nod to each other and sit at separate tables in the White Lion all afternoon, sometimes comment on the weather, whatever was in the headlines, or the plans for a national chain to take over the pub. He seemed neither happy nor unhappy, neither bored nor interested, and was never unnerved by silence. He just seemed to sit there living out his time. Only one subject could get him to talk at any length: the lives of the plants and insects in the garden of the old estate. After he'd given me a lesson to rival any naturalist, he'd sit back and sip his pint as my gaze began to blur and my unease faded. He knew not to bother talking to me in the evenings. I always wondered what he thought of me, the foreign boy with his laptop.

When I was younger I used to wonder how people so casually crossed the bridge between being alone to being in company, stepping forth from their own rooms to interact with others while apparently staying the same people they knew themselves to be. I wondered, for instance, how writers, at the literary events I sometimes went to, were able to talk to audiences about things they'd written in private as if real communication were taking place. I remember being impressed by a line from Cioran: *If we could see ourselves as others see us, we would vanish on the spot.* Sometimes I daydreamed about sending an experimental version of myself out into the world so I could observe him as he lived.

Sleepless again. But now a surprise: when I flip open the laptop, for a moment it's as if the words on the screen are someone else's. It gives me a brief feeling of freedom, like I'm able to reshape them as I please from a neutral vantage point. But then, when I return to them after stepping outside to smoke, they get jumbled up with my uncertain intentions and escape my grasp. I can't tell which are true and which are false, which are my own and which are not. Write for yourself, they say. For whom, exactly?

The double who stands beside me, watching on as I type, overseeing my work... I sometimes think, when I write, of what Gide had one of his characters say: *I am constantly getting outside myself, and as I watch myself act I can't understand how a person who acts is the same as the person who is watching him act, and who wonders in astonishment and doubt how he can be an actor and a watcher at the same moment.*

On Friday S. and I go to London, where she has a meeting, to spend the weekend with her old university friends. We take the bus to Norwich station, then the train to Liverpool Street. We work on the way down. As we approach the centre we pass colourful billboards in absurd contrast to the scrapyards and sooty blocks of flats in that peculiar grey-brown of British cities. The gigantic Westfield mall on one side, the City on the other. The train screeches down the littered tracks. Crowds heave and shove through rush hour. The noise knocks you back after the peace of the countryside. I sit in a pub and play with my phone while S. is in her meeting. Later we go out with her friends, none of whom I know, and wander from one rammed pub to the next until closing time. Faces blur into masks shouting at each other. What was his name again? And hers? Does it matter? Now I've woken at dawn in a dirty flat I don't know where, feeling porous and longing for tidy space, open air, silence.

Sunday. Tube, train, bus. A shower to wash off the grime, a nap, then a walk between the fields, through the woods, down to the river, while S. stays in the cottage and reads. It takes a long time to clear the sounds of rattling and clanking from my head. As I walk back, the clouds part before the setting sun. I sit on a log, roll a cigarette, and squint up at the sky.

A snippet of the day at last, I think, the day itself.

I look out over a long field of wheat. In the woods a pheasant hoots and claps his wings: it's breeding season. The sun sinks behind a stand of ash trees on the hill, its last rays spreading across the land and glinting off the dew on hay bales wrapped in plastic.

What *is* the day? Surely not a day like today, split between departures and destinations. Maybe it does have something to do with time, I tell myself, but the Earth's time. Planetary time. The flow of ocean currents, the drift of clouds, the shifting of seasons around the globe. Spend your time, they say. Make, allocate, invest time: as if time were ours to use as we please with no time left over. Meanwhile the day passes with no opinion of us.

Before heading home I stop at T.'s chicken coop. A bat flits out of the barn to feed on insects in the air. The sky is purple, ominous. I always contract a little at dawn and dusk, the blue hours, when you're either supposed to plan your day or take account of it. Early on, a voice says: how will you spend your time today? Then, later: what have you done today that's worth anything? I watch the hens peck at the ground behind the fence, joined by sparrows that haven't yet gone to roost. What do they care about how they've spent their day? They'll shuffle into their coop soon and sleep with ease. Will they dream, as they sit on their perches? They'll dream of sweetcorn and warm straw, perhaps: their favourite things. Dreams as natural as the flow of a stream.

Back at the cottage I warm some stew from the freezer and make a salad. All this pretentious talk about the day, I think to myself, when what I really want is to escape its tedium, watch old boxing matches on YouTube while S. does her online quizzes.

S. goes outside with a tin of sweetcorn for the chickens. A minute later I hear excited clucking and smile. How we love animals!

L. and M. arrive from Cambridge to stay with us for a few days. We play ping-pong in the village hall. Much laughter when the resident cat jumps up on the table and tries to bat the ball away. There's happiness in being with people.

But when L. and M. leave, life plods on as usual. S. does her remote work for a historical project and makes monthly trips to the university libraries in Norwich and Cambridge. I translate to the sound of cooing from pigeons on the eaves. The sound reminds me of endless afternoons in Denmark, growing up or waiting to. The evenings stretch out like clouds across the horizon...

Memories of last summer in Norwich, when it got bad. Before S. When for a long time I didn't talk to anyone except the Asian man in the off-licence.

At first I tried to walk myself out of it. In the beginning I'd walk for an hour or two, to the outskirts of the city and back. I'd stop in pubs, drink a pint here and there, sit half-listening to the jokes of builders in paint-spattered trousers. Warm drafts. Afternoon sunshine through dirty windows. I watched the drops run down the side of my pint glass. Dipped my fingers into the little puddles that gathered on the table.

Later, when I didn't have the energy to walk, I'd lie in bed thinking of ways to die. So this is what it's come to, I said to myself. You must be ill. Something in you is ill, something's grown in you, fed on you, and now look, you're ill in a dark room. It was almost a relief, to have only one thought, one sincere wish. Almost easier to be cornered and taken out of all fakery. This is what it comes down to, I thought: it's pure logic.

A hole. That was how it felt, like being in a hole, unable to look up. I'd wake at dawn, pulled suddenly out of a deep sleep, and start daydreaming of some fatal accident. A car crash, train wreck, meteor. Weeks went by like this.

But just as one has hidden weaknesses, one has hidden strengths. One day I drew a line that meant this stops here and stepped across it. I moved the line a little every day. It was simple: a simple question for once.

Sometimes a tiny shift of attention seemed to change everything, or rather illuminate what was already there, like a light turned on in a room of shadows. I started walking again, and now I could go further, out of the city, through woods, along lanes, into the country.

One day I came across a small medieval church. A chicken bobbed through the tall grass in the graveyard, which overlooked a rapeseed field. I walked down the path, opened the bird grille and the heavy wooden door, and stepped into the cool musty nave. It was empty. I sat for a long time on a pew where the light came in through a stained-glass window. I felt like a speck inside—what? I sensed an overfacing power that shook me out of myself: something wholly other. It withdrew, and left me with a strange hope.

The days are getting warmer. I've started exercising again. I work in the garden, ride to the farm shop. We cycle up to the north coast, chain our bikes to a tree and walk through the wood on a sandy path. S. stops here and there to open her wildlife book and identify some plant or insect. We chat without paying attention to our surroundings, emerge from the wood to find ourselves before a wide-open view: on one side the sea and the sky, a vast canvas of blues, whites, and greys; on the other, scrapes and grassy dunes spreading out inland.

It's moments like these I want to write about. Moments when you're stopped on your way and made to see where you are with new eyes. As when you work on a problem that seems unsolvable and all of a sudden the answer comes: it was there all along, why couldn't I see it? Or when a situation makes you act in a way that confronts you with yourself, and it's as though the past opens up: so *that's* why I've always behaved like that, now I see. Or when, in novels, moments of insight arise from the events of the story to make the story seem almost redundant. I daydream of a book containing only such passages, something like Stephen Hero's book of epiphanies, or a collection of Woolf's *little daily miracles, illuminations, matches struck unexpectedly in the dark.*

I cycle, run, swim. To get in shape, to feel strength and confidence slowly build, find muscles reappearing, is a delight and a relief from all kinds of physical and mental ills. Trivial problems fall away and things lighten a little, become more endurable.

The pine grove at Wells-next-the-Sea. Its springy floor of brown needles is crossed by twisted grey roots. We stop to look at a stand of ragworts crawling with caterpillars. Cinnabars, says S., who knows more about these things than I do. We go down to the beach and make for the water, dry razor clams crunching under our feet. When we're settled on our towels we watch the waders pick at the sand. S. points out how pretty the oystercatchers look in flight, their black wings flashing white Vs. She follows them with her binoculars. I run along the shoreline to Holkham beach, past dogwalkers and horse riders in jodhpurs. A tern folds its wings and plunges into the sea, emerging with a gleaming fish in its talons. I do some push-ups, brave the steely water, then run back to S. We return home to find a neat line of ants from the front door to the kitchen, up the cupboard and onto the counter, where our strawberries lie oozing in a bowl, covered in a feasting swarm.

On the way to the shops today I passed a blackbird lying on the pavement with a broken wing. It flailed about helplessly, trying to get up. I walked past it because I was hungry, thought better of it and went back to do the manly thing and put it out of its misery. As they say. I remembered my grandfather telling me stories about such mercies performed as a matter of course on his farm. It was worse than I thought, not at all a matter of course for me. The bird felt like a tiny broken umbrella as it thrashed in my grip. When I wrung its neck it squirted out a thin white stream of excrement. Its eyes turned glassy as it went limp and its beak opened up, unhinged. I put it in a bin and lost my appetite.

Some days it seems impossible to write. My words are traitorous: they turn on me and make me cringe. They become the words of others, strange judges, using me even as I think I use them. Kafka's final diary entry:

> More and more fearful as I write. It is understandable. Every word, twisted in the hands of the spirits—this twist is their characteristic gesture—becomes a spear turned against the speaker. Most especially a remark like this. And so ad infinitum. The only consolation would be: it happens whether you like or no. And what you like is of infinitesimally little help. More than consolation is: you too have weapons.

What weapons did he mean?

In Beckett, too, words turn against the narrator: *How they must hate me! Ah a nice state they have me in — but still I'm not their creature (not quite, not yet). It's a poor trick that consists in ramming a set of words down your gullet on the principle that you can't bring them up without being branded as belonging to their breed.* What was Beckett's weapon against the traitorous menace of words, what was his defence against unfreedom? Let writing lead you into complete incomprehension. Fail better. Not in order to succeed but to make your failure total. Is this really what I want? Haven't I tried? Where did it lead me?

Blanchot, like the early Beckett, saw writing as a submission to an obscure, incessant murmur outside meaning, there being no alternative. The writer for him was always astray, always in errancy: *The writer belongs to a language spoken by no one, addressed to no one, which has no centre and reveals nothing. He may believe that he affirms himself in this language, but what he affirms is entirely empty of self.*

Words flow through you in a ceaseless stream whether you like it or not, it's true. Then try to find yourself in them: stem the flow for a moment, just as you'd try to find yourself in a crowd of people going different ways and saying different things. Start like that.

Then what? Small acts of kindness that make the day real. I love you, says S., seriously, as she chops vegetables. For a second I'm not sure who she means. T. brings us a couple of his rib-eye steaks. I thank him overenthusiastically. We have to help each other out out here, he says, and walks back to his farm.

Early morning. A screen of condensation on the window. A few drops break away and leave clear wet lines as they fall. Outside a fog hangs over the field. I sip my tea, empty-headed, until the fog thins into wisps and evaporates into the day. S. comes out of the bedroom, stretches, smiles, and touches my arm.

The difficulty of balancing inner and outer, self and other. We move in and out of ourselves. I begin to see the meaning of living in this landscape, formed through centuries of interaction between humans and nature. The Broads, a shifting network of tidal rivers, lakes, and marshes, began life as medieval peat mines. As sea levels rose, the pits and hollows flooded despite attempts to drain the land (the area is crisscrossed by dykes and dotted with ruined and restored pumping mills). Today, the coastal and inland nature reserves, surrounded by monocultural fields and built-up areas, are home to countless plant and animal species that would be threatened without patient conservation. Seaside embankments preserve habitats of migratory birds. Careful reed-cutting creates environments for local fauna, especially invertebrates. Biomanipulation and dredging restore lakes; livestock grazing prevents re-forestation and makes room for rare plants. All to allow for variation and growth, as when we weed our gardens to let the plants and flowers grow, blossom, and attract pollinators.

The bats hang under the bridge like bunches of grapes. Hard not to shudder, as when one sees rats crawling over each other or a snake slithering across a river. But now in the gloaming they come alive, flit back and forth between their roost and the river to drink and to feed on insects. The water ripples where one has grabbed a bug just above the surface or taken a sip on the wing. They must be Daubenton's, says S., they like water. The bats' calls start as questions thrown into the void: pulses that bounce off walls, off water and trees, and back into the creatures' nervous systems, which in turn recreate the world around them so intimately they can catch tiny insects invisible to us as we watch from the bank. What to us is a confusion of flapping wings is to the bats a high-precision hunt. Almost blind, they're nevertheless at home in their environment in ways we can only piece together from outside.

Heavy with homesickness for being: ill-adapted. In my heaviness the moment passes me by. I'm looking for it in these scattered words. Is it looking for me too, the moment, calling me into itself? Does it need my words to come to itself? But it's been and gone and I'm passing my time in detours. Then—miracle—the words come together and lift me into it.

A walk before lunch. I sit on the stump of a tree and write a note on my phone. The screen reflects the sky as I write, partly obscuring my words. When I name a thing it comes alive for an instant, then sinks back into itself. These words really should be varying shades between black and white, appearing and disappearing on the screen. And yet they seem to be making their way towards something. Towards what?

The wisdom of certain everyday phrases. We speak of being in the moment and of pregnant moments. We speak of the fullness of time, of a time that's ripe. Beautiful phrase: the fullness of time. What does it mean? In everyday language, when something happens in the fullness of time it happens at a time that has finally come, a time of the fulfilment of some event. Something comes into its own, something time has ripened. For the early Christians it had to do with the first and second coming of Christ, and the coming to pass of God's plan at decisive moments in history. But what if it were taken to refer not to a past or future event so much as to time *itself*? What if the fullness of time referred not to a time that's ripe *for* something but to a time that's ripe with itself, that fulfils itself in the moment?

If the moment is the revelation of the fullness of time, it can't be part of everyday time. It can't simply be one of a series of separate nows, but rather the felt instant that opens your present out to the future and gives your past meaning—only to withdraw again.

Karl Jaspers: *The atom of time is of course nothing, but the moment is everything.* Then how to hold this moment as it emerges, as it lets you emerge with it? It's bigger than you, and once reached can't be commanded. How to find it? How to stay in it? Endure it?

T.'s kittens have been weaned, so now we have five little rascals tumbling around in a big cardboard box lined with newspapers: mewling, hissing, sleeping, and scratching us when we handle them. Their eyes are changing colour. We put on our winter gloves, pick them up and feed them cat food covered in worming medicine we bought from the vet in the next village. When we fry T.'s steaks we treat the kittens to a few slivers. They slowly start to trust us and want to be let out. S. puts a sign on the road and an ad on the internet. Her efforts are surprisingly successful. People come from far and wide, mostly mothers, two of them with excited children. I let S. deal with them. We keep one kitten, a male. Except for a white patch on its forehead, it's black like a rook. It seems to belong to this place. It's sleeping on my lap as I write.

But look at these pages. Occasional paragraphs splintered with white spaces. Again the entries split apart as soon as I look at them. I'm outside my words. I try to gather my thoughts like someone who stops up in a shop and tries to remember what he went in for, but it's hopeless.

Try again. Write what's in front of you. Very well. The trees are in full bloom and the undergrowth is spreading across the paths in the woods. Snails leave their glistening trails on our flagstones and unfailingly find their way back to our lettuce after we throw them into the bushes. They have a sense of direction, says S., like an inbuilt GPS. She won't let me put salt out to be rid of them.

Good. Try again.

T.'s getting on; he stoops now. We'll have to help more around the farm. He still keeps a handful of beef heifers in his field, which he brings into the cowshed in winter. The windows are caked in cobwebs. In the hay-barn are stacks of twine-bound bales beside a mound of silage. The barn on the other side of the courtyard is full of rusty tools and machinery, a small silo, and a tractor. The floor is scattered with grain and the air hangs warm and stale. Dust plays in the shafts of light let in through cracks in the wooden walls. The old wheat field is fallow and has turned into a meadow with wildflowers and wavy grasses that ripple like water in wind. The fruit and vege-table patches are tangled with brambles. Time has slowed for T. too. He still gets help from a couple of local farm workers, but it's too much for him: he's thinking of sell-ing up. Some of his regular customers—butchers, caterers, market stalls—have shut down, unable to compete with the supermarket chains and their nationwide suppliers.

S. makes T. a cake using some of his rhubarb. She has an idea. With his grudging permission she takes a plank from a pile in the barn and a handsaw and makes a neat painted sign above our door: THE ROOKERY. She puts out another sign on the roadside saying FRUIT, VEG, EGGS FOR SALE— KNOCK AT THE ROOKERY, sets up a Facebook page and adds us to a direct farm sales website. We now keep T.'s excess produce in our pantry. We eat and pickle some, sell some, and give him whatever money we make. We also help weed and water his patches.

Drizzle. In the morning a van delivers my new bike. The old one was heavy and creaky. What to do with it? Deal with that later.

Despite the weather I cycle to the seaside in half the time. The low tide exposes a slick sandbank on which tiny crabs scuttle between pebbles and bladderwrack. This stretch of the coast is a world away from the northern part. In fact the Norfolk coastline is as clear a demonstration of the British class system as you could wish for. To the east, Great Yarmouth with its familiar story: once a rich port and Victorian holiday resort, now one of the most deprived towns in the country after decades of budget airlines and package holidays, and a spiral of unemployment and neglect as the regional cities have gentrified and pushed those on the margins further out. Here are discount stores, gaming arcades, fast-food outlets. Litter everywhere. The dogs of choice are bull terriers and westies. To the north, at a suitable distance from the caravan parks, second homes in tasteful muted colours and Range Rovers have replaced the old fishermen's cottages and carts. The beaches are cleaner. The pubs have Michelin stickers on their doors, and cocker spaniels and labradors lie obediently under the tables.

To the pub in Rockland after a long walk around the marshes. The locals eye me as I approach the bar, but I'm used to that by now. Often I find they'll loosen up and joke with you if you're reasonably friendly and confident, or at least act like you are. That's when I have to concentrate: it can be hard to understand them, especially when they're drunk. After hearing my accent, a man with a weather-beaten face and missing teeth asks me where I'm from. I'm used to that too. I give him my usual line and ask if he lives around here. He tells me he's moored at the pier and has lived on his boat for ten years, cruising up and down the rivers. You must've met a lot of tourists over the years, I say. Oh all sorts, he says, from all over: Germany, the Netherlands, even China. He says it's not for everyone, this life. It gets bleak in the winter. But he loves being out there on his own. He can go wherever he wants and stop at all the pubs. As so often when I talk to older men in pubs, I get the sense that there's a troubled past behind the things he says. His accent is so thick I have to ask him to repeat himself a couple of times. I say I've heard the tides can be tricky. He nods and tells me about the treacherous Breydon Water, the estuary at

Yarmouth where the rivers Bure, Yare, and Waveney lead into the sea. He says it gets a lot calmer towards the north and rolls his eyes. They got everything better up there, he says, but I like docking down this way, you can talk to people, cahnya. I nod, then hear a ping. I put my pint on the bar and pull out my phone. A job. I excuse myself and look around for a sign showing the pub's wifi password. When I find it I sit at a table and pull my laptop out of my bag. The text hasn't been taken yet. I look through it, click CLAIM, get the usual tiny thrill when it appears under JOBS IN PROGRESS, then immediately feel the need to go home and start it.

Clearing out the drawers around the house, I find old charger cables, out-of-date medications, a Kindle we've never used, a toothbrush, a pregnancy test kit, letters, stones and figurines that S. says are important to her, and an old notebook of mine. It's mostly blank. There are lines here and there, written in pubs, before the last time writing fizzled out:

> Frightening thought: you're an impostor who doesn't know the extent of his own imposture. Worse, the imposture that stands between you and the world, that *is* your world.

> The fear that everything is outside of itself. Buildings, trees, people, all scattered among each other, other than themselves. Nothing can come to itself because nothing really is. The world is one giant diversion from itself, an error.

> The fear that everything is the same. That you're a thing among things, emerging from sameness only to be swallowed by the same again. The days pass under the usual blind sky, unable to change or begin. Time, slowed to a crawl. Time, endless.

> The pub toilet. Haze. The face in the mirror can't see itself. You go back to the table and hear your mouth saying words, mouthing lies. Sudden plunges. Sinkholes of time.

But now a new urgency: shed all that like old scales. Find new words.

The cat—we call him Rookie—rolls onto my notebook and bats away my pen with beautiful disregard.

In the evenings the rooks and crows congregate in the air, split apart and come together, then suddenly settle in the trees as night falls. Who knows what they're saying to each other as they fill the sky with their raucous calls? Are they gossiping, fighting, finding mates? Yet they can also talk like us, mimic our speech. They can recognise our faces, bring us gifts or take revenge on us, even through generations. They're social, cunning, adaptable.

Early humans, it's said, learned about their surroundings from corvids. Interactions between hunter-gatherers and corvids may even have led to a kind of cultural co-evolution: the birds may have changed their behaviour to lead people to large prey in hope of a meal of leftovers, and people in turn may have changed their behaviour to understand and follow the birds. Our close association with them, and the need to defend our food from them, may have refined our own co-operation and communication. Later cultures saw them as living symbols of natural and divine forces—sometimes light, sometimes primal darkness. Crows and ravens carried messages from the gods or had sacred ties to the sun. They were bearers of meaning in the world. The negative connotations of corvids largely came about with the rise of industrial agriculture and the sight of crows picking at corpses on battlefields. They became seen as threats to profit and birds of ill omen—to us. But these kinds of physical and symbolic links between people and animals have long since broken. Animals are now mostly products or sources of entertainment, to be used and segregated, or only let into our world as pets. Even so, they're still essentially the same: *both like and unlike man,* as John Berger wrote. They still gaze at us from afar, from the silence of the day, and before their gazes we're more alone than ever. We look to them to find the secret of our origins but they don't answer us. Maybe their non-answer is the answer: find the secret for yourself.

The faith involved even in typing a sentence, this sentence. Something takes hold. Something happens in spite of everything, something you're responsible for. Though you may never arrive you're approaching, and some truth may be given to you in your approach. Is this the weapon that's given to you in writing, the hidden strength you need?

Within the seemingly endless stream of words, the moment calls me into service to name it. The double who stood beside me now draws back in. The space between us fills with time. Joy.

Words are worn out, the moment and the day too, barely there—yet as full as ever. A new time to listen and respond. Strange route to what's already here, waiting to be summoned.

I've bought a homemade kayak from wild-haired N. We met when I lived in Norwich. He moved to Kirkwood, bought and fixed up an old farmhouse, and convinced S. and I to move out here too. He moulded the kayak from fibreglass in his old barn. He makes all kinds of things there, mainly sculptures, and he's experimenting with making cheap, non-polluting sculpting material from glues and wood-chips he gets from the local tree surgeon. He stomps down the mixture in buckets. Don't come too close, he told me through his mask when I went to see him: it smells pretty rank. At the other end of the barn is a smelter, as well as moulds, gloves, welding equipment, lots of tools. In the garden are swans' necks carved from branches and wire sculptures in the trees. By the road is a sign: SCULPTURES MADE TO ORDER. N. helps me carry the kayak to the river. I plunk down awkwardly and almost tip over. It's wobbly. Eventually I settle in the seat, get my hips and shoulders into the right rhythm, and paddle awhile over swaying river plants. Dozens of blue damselflies skit across the water. I manage to turn round, paddle back, and leave the kayak under a willow tree.

We bike to Strumpshaw Fen. From the low-lying path the pleasure boats on the river seem to glide over the reeds.

In the hide, S. points out a marsh harrier flapping errat-
ically above the reedbed and a cormorant standing on a
post with outstretched wings, like some strange idol pre-
siding over this man-managed reserve. Above the meadows, shrieking swifts feed on mists of insects they'll soon
carry back south in their bellies. A partridge hops along
the path in front of us. We point and laugh at its panicky
prance, but there's no comedy in nature. It hides at the
edge of the reedbed, where it stops as we walk up to it and
looks back at us in what seems like fear. Sometimes you
only see how different from us wild animals are when
you get close to them: the black beads in its head hardly
look like eyes, its richly detailed plumage isn't for us.

Rilke:

With all their eyes, creatures look out
into the Open. Only our eyes are
ingrown, and surround beings
like traps, encircling their free going-forth.
What is outside, we know only from the
gazes of animals; for even the young child
we turn about, so that he is forced to see forms
backwardly, not the Open, which
is so deep in the animal's face.

Rookie's growing fast but retaining the juvenile white patch on his forehead as pet cats sometimes do. We play with him, toying about with a ball of string, which gets tangled among the chairs as he zooms around. He's testing his strength against the world, mainly the sofa and us, using his claws and teeth. I have mixed feelings about keeping him as a pet.

I'm helping T. collect eggs in the coop when he leaves and returns with a shotgun and a box of shells and hands them to me. Oi cahn see good enough to aim new more, he says. Yew take tha, and if yew see a fox, shoot tha on soight. I tell him I don't have a licence and have never shot anything, but he waves off my protests. I put the gun and shells aside and bring them back to the cottage when we're done. I try to be casual about it but am unsure of where to leave them. I decide to lean the gun against a wall in the corner of the living room and put away the shells in the chest of drawers. S. is uneasy.

I get a job—a corporate strategy—with a deadline at ten in the morning, so I decide to stay up late to finish it rather than get up early. When I'm done I can't sleep. Awake until three now: a new record. The sleeping pill doesn't take. The mind won't give itself up. It tears into the same old thoughts like a machine until at last it's released from itself and sinks into blackness. Must have happened near dawn.

"I'm not myself today." Who or what then? Woolf: *I see myself as a fish in a stream; deflected; held in place; but cannot describe the stream.*

When I was younger I felt often as if the current of another life, the success I should have been in the world, flowed over me, pushed me this way and that, or left me stranded somewhere or other. What's Woolf's stream now but the flow of capital and the stories of success it uses to seduce us, having demolished the old stories of our lives? All day I translate business texts to make money to pay our inflated rent. We're degraded by capital, a force as concrete as the foundations under our house and as abstract as stock indices rolling down a screen. It reaches us even out here in the country, of course, infiltrates our lives no matter where we go. It owns us, makes us want to degrade ourselves before it, mocks these words, tells me I don't understand it because I'm not living in the real world, which is its world, a world that seeks to swallow all alternatives. We try to straighten out the twisted postures this life has forced us into so we can walk, breathe, think. We try to gather strength to unlearn its false joys and happy endings, to see through the screens it erects against the day.

Some of the texts I translate talk about brand narratives and the power of storytelling to create an authentic relationship with the consumer. The more compelling your story is to the consumer the more competitive *you'll* be, they say. It seems everyone needs a successful story.

T.'s cows come trotting over when they see me. We've gotten to know each other. I bite off chunks of apples and feed them into their drooling muzzles. I like to feel their hot breath on my hand. They're curious creatures: they follow me along their side of the fence even when I don't have anything for them, and stand and look at me in puzzlement when I whistle a tune. These animals have a story: from the shed and field to the slaughterhouse and supermarket.

The patterns on a cow's muzzle are as unique as human fingerprints. Scientists have developed a biometric system for big farms that scans muzzle prints and identifies cattle more efficiently than branding and ear notching. This makes it easier to trace each cow from birth to slaughter and out through the supply chain.

In the afternoon I take a book to the garden and sit in the lawnchair. As soon as I've got comfortable I'm bombarded by an army of flying insects. I look behind me and see a swarm on the ground, in the plants, on the wall, mingling with ants that pour up from the cracks between the flagstones. Rookie bounds out of a bush and leaps up to swat at them. I stand, flick them off my shoulders, off my arms and legs, and step on them. But they keep coming, massing around a crack beside the kitchen door. Are they attacking the ants? I go inside to get the insect spray, spray the air and ground. I wait a while, then sit back down and start reading again, dozens of insects twitching on the ground around me. When S. returns from the shop and sees the scene from the kitchen window, she comes out and asks me what I've done. They were everywhere, I say, attacking the ants. She explains that they *were* ants: winged males and virgin queens on their nuptial flight. They have wings, she says, they were looking for each other. Some of them might have come from another nest. They fly at the same time, she says; I saw some on the way back. The big ones are the queens. Didn't you see them? She gives me a disappointed look and goes inside to put the shopping away. I sweep up the dead ants, go inside to check the facts online, and find, for instance, that the queens can continue to lay eggs for up to twenty years after mating in the air. I feel rather ashamed of the little massacre I've committed.

We're sitting in the garden working on our laptops, waving away flies, when N. surprises us with a beautiful rook he's made from twisted black wire. He's even scraped the base of the bill to distinguish it from a crow. He refuses money but I go into the cottage, get what cash I have and stuff it into his pocket. I have to grapple with him to keep it in there. We end up lying on the lawn. S. brings us beers and hangs the rook on a branch of the oak tree, where it turns slowly in the wind. I give N. my old bike. He says he'll use it to make a sculpture. Before he leaves, S. gives him some eggs and vegetables to take home.

One of those clear, fresh mornings when I swear I can smell the tang of sea in the air. S. is sceptical. She and I move about the cottage each feeling the other's presence. We speak, or don't: speech or silence, it's all the same. When she goes out to the garden I sense her absence even if I haven't heard her leave. She says she's felt this too. In her academic way she tells me about a study which showed that when couples live together they begin to mirror one another physiologically. Their heart rates, breathing, and brainwaves synchronise, as when our footsteps fall in with those of the person we're walking with.

Noise weighs on me, even out here. The right words come only in stillness. When the pigeons aren't cooing, when the cat isn't scratching something, customers aren't knocking on the door for eggs, delivery vans aren't rolling by to T.'s farm—then something takes hold that's mine yet not mine. Words born of silence, returning to a kind of silent saying.

The field just before dawn, still half-hidden in night. The birds start their territorial music. Each element of the landscape slowly reappears from the murk: the molehills on the field, a pair of rabbits, the poles of the fence, the trees in the distant wood. The crows wake and fly from their nests. But as the daylight separates things out, it also reveals their interconnections. The landscape makes sense, it's as if it's *happening*, and I'm happening with it as I stand looking out the window, slowly waking. Then I sit with a yawn, turn on the computer to check for new work. The internet plays up again, and the spell is broken, as they say.

Rookie now seems interested in us only when we're doing physical work around the house, especially cleaning the floor. I wonder if it's an old farm instinct: people working on the ground might stir up creatures to eat. He's already chasing rodents and birds. Soon he'll start looking for a mate; we haven't had him neutered. He's still a little wild, still hisses. Yet it's hard not to bother him as he sits on the windowsill, shiny as a beetle—to try to make him come to me, to do my bidding.

Herons stand on the riverbank, gazing into the water. Solemn, hieratic. I never see them catch anything. In the evenings we hear the snarls of rutting roebucks. Like the cries of the foxes and pheasants there's nothing cute about the sound. It's bestial. Now is the time to fight and mate. Over dinner at the cottage, T. tells a story from many years ago when a friend of his in North Norfolk found two red deer stags with their antlers locked. They must've been lying there for a while, he says, because one of them had died and been partly consumed. He takes a sip of beer. The glass looks small in his great calloused hand. Bloody fohxes, he says in his singsong, a yew shot one yet? Crows too, I imagine, I say to get him off the subject. He nods. Em crews'll eat anything. He says he held down the living stag while his friend cut off part of an antler with a handsaw. A were a roight palaver, he says, it were raw an orl. They had to run away as the stag thrashed to free itself from its rival and finally bounded back into the woods. An noh a word of thanks, says T., taking a bite of his lambchop.

Today I took the kayak out again. I thought I'd mastered it until the seat started sliding off and I fell into the cold water in the middle of the river. I ended up having to fling the seat into the reeds with one hand while holding onto the paddle and kayak with the other. I couldn't get back onboard because the kayak tipped too much under my weight, so I manoeuvred down the river for what seemed a long time, the water plants curling around my feet, until I got to a bank where I could climb up. I was frightened despite myself, and it was instructive to be taught again how small a shift is needed before we're out of our element, floundering like an animal driven from its natural habitat. It was impossible to bring the kayak through the brush so I left it there by the water. I almost lost a shoe in the suck and my legs and arms are scratched.

It's similar with moods: one small shift and you can be plunged into a different mood and feel like a different person. I wake up happy, spend the morning joking with S. while making tuna salad, eat too much, take a nap, and wake up heavy-headed and irritable. I snap at S., catch myself, apologise, and decide to go for a run to shake off the temper. I notice an overgrown bridle path I hadn't seen before and decide to head down it. Nettles sting my legs. I stop, look at the ground for a moment, breathing heavily, then rip a branch off a tree to thrash the nettles aside. Hogweed, too, and all the other shit I can't name. Pigeons flutter from the boughs above me, their wings whistling in alarm, and something I can't see scurries out of the bushes. Finally I break the branch across the same tree I ripped it from.

No writing for two weeks. Only translating other people's words, finding ways to formulate other people's half-baked sentences, mostly about how to make more money. Try again: what's in front of you? That I'm distracted, derailed. Too much of a burden to go back into myself in order to get out of myself. All I want to do is disappear, drink, have nothing to do with anything or anyone. The gun isn't a wholesome thing to have in the house on days like these. Try for S.'s sake, then. Why should she have to deal with your moods? Read that paragraph again, the one that made you happier than ever: *The faith involved even in typing a sentence, this sentence...*

Odd place to be, where only writing can lift your spirits.

Emerson:

> Our moods do not believe in each other. Today I am full of thoughts and can write what I please. I see no reason why I should not have the same thought, the same power of expression, tomorrow. What I write, whilst I write it, seems the most natural thing in the world; but yesterday I saw a dreary vacuity in this direction in which now I see so much; and a month hence, I doubt not, I shall wonder who he was that wrote so many continuous pages. Alas for this infirm faith, this will not strenuous, this vast ebb of a vast flow!

To write yourself out of distraction. Who has the time? What would T. say about these little inner struggles? He must have his own.

First hints of autumn. The Earth is easing into its great rest. The mornings and evenings are cooler, the dawn chorus quieter. The birds that haven't left are conferring about their journeys. *Zugunruhe*, the Germans call it, migratory unrest. The refined smell of smoking leaves reaches our garden from T.'s burn barrel. The farmers are ploughing their fields, their tractors trailed by flocks of gulls after worms.

Uneven time between seasons, quietly dramatic, like the sky between daytime and night. I thought autumn was coming but summer wants to linger; the sun still has life to give. The berries, apples, and pears are ripening, and we found a fig tree in the cemetery. Its bulbous, infolded fruits are growing softer to the touch, more and more like breasts, and turning from green to mottled purple.

Later. A swollen grey sky. Then cloudburst. Sodden earth. Water runs like cables along the side of the path and tumbles out of the drainpipe into the rain barrel at the corner of the cottage, reminding me I need to borrow T.'s ladder and clean the gutters.

We've eaten so many blackberries we're almost sick of them. Brambles grow like weeds here, crowding out other plants, covering fences, paths, ruined churches. Their fruits vary greatly in taste since different varieties grow beside each other. One is luscious, the next sour. Some dissolve as we pick them, staining our hands, others are hard to the touch. They range from yellow to deep purple. Like animals, we quickly learn which are likely to taste good.

The endurance of animals. They bear the world in ways we can't. Like animals we're thrown into the need to attend to our bodies and surroundings—to survive—but we also hear the call of our moral being, of conscience, which is impossible to heed at every moment. I work long hours, make some money, think I've satisfied every demand I face, think I can rest, but it's still there, more urgent than before, this annoying call to go back to yourself, to justify your existence and mean something beyond your capacity to earn money; in my case by writing this journal. But I get bored and crave distraction. Or resent the call and find cryptic ways to put it out of my mind. Rookie, meanwhile, loafs in the sun, content to be left alone.

Moments of full attention require moments of diversion, of play. But when time itself is scattered to the winds of capital and our attention exploited and turned into distraction, we risk losing ourselves in detours. Our play is more and more commodified along paths set out for us by systems that control our behaviour—new and interesting until you see they lead nowhere. And what's left but uncreative boredom when manufactured novelty ceases to fascinate, when the new sinks back into sameness and we've all seen through it? How do we recover ourselves? I think of N.'s rook: an act of generosity with no end but the joy of creating and giving.

Mark Fisher:

> The tiniest event can tear a hole in the grey curtain of reaction which has marked the horizons of possibility under capitalist realism. From a situation in which nothing can happen, suddenly anything is possible again.

I sit on the sofa and read beside Rookie. I come across a line that makes me stare into space. I return to it, then stare into space again. My thoughts roam around some just-out-of-reach idea or feeling (or a memory of an idea or feeling) but my energies peter out until I realise I'm gazing at nothing, thinking about nothing. I annoy myself, return to the book, force myself to read a few more lines, but can't take them in. I reach out to pet the cat. He stands, stretches, and hops off the sofa.

Cats don't meow to each other except as kittens. The territorial sounds they make as adults are quite different, more animal. The meowing of domesticated cats is a behaviour they've learned, perhaps from human babies, like walking around our legs. They also have an especially annoying solicitation purr. Rookie doesn't meow and is still mostly nocturnal, as he would be in the wild. He wakes us up at night by knocking things over and biting our toes.

Bare branches against a sky the colour of cigarette smoke. Cold damp air. Leaves flushing red. Autumn setting in now: dusk all day. The usual sense of slow decline and foreboding. How will I get through it this year?

All is seared with trade; bleared, smeared with toil, wrote Hopkins from deep inside an industrial England spreading its greyness across the world.

I remember the first of many manual jobs I did when I was younger, in the year before I went to university, working in the supermarket in Denmark. It was the kind of store that could offer the lowest possible prices by streamlining transportation and minimising staff. Naturally it was the busiest in town. I was on my feet all day except at lunch and when I covered the tills: I cleaned, moved pallets, loaded the cardboard baler, ordered products, ordered people about, made sure the staff counted their cash correctly after their shifts. Twice a week I had to open at five in the morning to take deliveries from lorries that had been loaded overnight, then do a twelve-hour shift. I liked the physical work. It helped me. It focused my mind, and I slept better. But if the work was a virtuous circle for me in the short run, in the long run it was just a grind that others higher up profited from far more than my co-workers and I. It was a constant cycle of goods coming in at one end and going out the other, of stacking shelves and tidying up to keep the store looking the same. Soon after I started I'd been sent to the chain's main logistics hub on Zealand along with other new employees from around the region, where we were given a tour by an enthusiastic HR duo. The workers on the floor looked less enthused than our hosts. The place was huge, like an aerospace institute, and I started to get a sense of the sheer scale of the mechanisms that ran under things I'd always taken for granted, everyday activities of suburban life like driving, shopping, eating at a café, simply walking around: the vast production facilities, global transport networks, flows of investment capital, strict corporate hierarchies: the countless acts of violence against people and the environment that made all these things possible.

Hopkins again: *For all this, nature is never spent / There lives the dearest freshness deep down things.* We bring home our bounty from the fig tree. The fruits are the size of S.'s fist and heavy, their rubbery skin bulging with goodness. We devour two apiece on the way back, ripping open the almost obscenely red flesh with our teeth and wiping our hands on the grass and our jeans. What was it D.H. Lawrence called them? I look it up: *womb-fibrilled.* The way autumn fruits ripen, come into their own while everything else wilts: remember this, hold on to it.

Fig trees are pollinated by a certain species of wasp. The adult female will crawl into a fig, breaking her wings as she does so, then lay her eggs and die. Her offspring will mate with each other and the flightless males will eat tunnels through the fig's skin before dying inside it. The young females will then collect the pollen and fly out of the tunnels to find a fig of their own, while the tree slowly transforms the dead mother and males into fruit.

I love to watch S. when she returns from T.'s chicken coop with a basket full of eggs and boxes and carefully— attentively!—washes the eggs with the hose, dries them with a rag, and puts them in the boxes one by one. There are fewer eggs now that the summer glut is over, but we've made some money from roadside sales.

The brambles are withering, their berries shrinking into hard bitter beads. S. has bought a field guide to foraging. We take it with us on a walk and pick mushrooms and elderberries. We make omelettes with the mushrooms and S. puts the elderberries in a crumble.

I decide to take out the gun to try to shoot some wood pigeons. Does it need oiling? I put some of my bicycle oil on it. I try to remember all the things my grandfather told me about hunting with his dog, near his farm in Denmark. As a child I always longed to join him, but he only let me shoot his air rifles. Now's my chance. He had a contraption he would stick in the ground, the top of which folded out into a seat. Our plastic garden chair will have to do. He also had binoculars, heavy and covered in leather, which I used to play with, adjusting their sights and turning them over in my hands. I borrow the plastic ones S. has for birdwatching. MADE IN CHINA, it says on the side.

I shoot a couple of shells into the air to test the recoil and the spray of the pellets. Then I go to the woods at the edge of the field and sit down facing away from the trees, load the gun, cock it and keep it pointed up, as my grandfather taught me. I wait for an age. It's cold and boring; I wish I'd brought my hat. I start thinking about other things. Finally a pigeon flaps out. I start, stand, and shoot almost randomly into the air. Other birds emerge, there's a great commotion behind and in front of me. I see a pair of pigeons, take aim, and one of them drops! I walk over to it: happily, it's dead. That's enough for today, I decide. I bring everything back to the cottage to S. like a proud hunter. For some reason carrying a dead bird isn't unpleasant this time, and S. is on board with it.

My grandmother used to prepare the birds my grandfather shot. I remember her showing me how to remove the entrails in the sink. She had a vat in the barn where she would dip the pigeons and pheasants in boiling water before defeathering them. S. and I watch a YouTube video that explains how to do it and I roast the pigeon with potatoes and braise red cabbage with butter, sugar, and vinegar, the Danish way. It's a lot of work for a small meal, we agree. I tell her I probably won't bother doing it again.

S. goes to London for a conference. I have one of my cleaning fits. I take everything out of the pantry and fridge and clean the shelves, soak the shower curtain, hoover and mop the floors, wipe the kitchen cupboards. Rookie's annoyed at being woken up in every room. He gives me sleepy little growls as he pads off. I clean after I've finished a big job or when I'm feeling out of place, to feel at home again or at least maintain the ecology of the household.

The earth reclaims things so quickly out here. The floor gets dirty, the cottage gets colonised by insects, by rising damp. There's a Danish word for what happens to a house that hasn't been lived in for a while: it gets *jordslået*, literally earth-hit. Cold seeps into its walls, it gets mouldy and mildewed, loses its homely borders as the landscape starts to absorb it.

Like many young people—she's younger than me—S. gets wanderlust. They're tired of home, want more out of life. When I was younger I almost felt envious of those who had the urge to travel, of the rootedness it grew from. They took their homes with them, after all, when they left, even if they resented them, and they could always go back, and usually did. For people like me who grew up in different countries, it doesn't work that way. It can't. You make your home where you can, or you drift somewhere else.

After twenty years in Norfolk I'm still a furriner, as they say here. For one thing, my accent sets me apart every time I open my mouth. The locals, who are often suspicious of foreigners, accept your presence but don't actively welcome you; they tend to leave you alone. Which suits me fine. There's a freedom in being an outsider. The British class system, for instance, doesn't touch me as profoundly as people who were raised in this country. I can wonder at its absurdities from the outside, at the way everything and everyone here is marked by it, so that no British person can escape it even if they travel and settle abroad.

But doesn't every home contain an element of the foreign? After all, the homely is defined by the unhomely, takes its meaning from it. Dwellings, like countries, are defined by their differences from everything that's outside them, from which they're separated by walls and fences. And a home itself can suddenly seem alien, after a row with a lover, for instance, or a break-in, or missing a month's rent... In any case, aren't we more uprooted than ever? Every home is now connected to networks that break down the borders between home and elsewhere. Capital extends its reach by the day, the virtual consumes the natural. We move about in unshared spaces, unnatural states of displacement.

Homeless at home. What choice then but to try to find a home in homelessness? To return to where you find yourself. Home in the midst of displacement. More you than you, like that morning when you woke with the landscape at dawn.

T.'s field is getting muddy. It's time to bring the cows into the shed for the winter. T.'s helpers are busy, so he comes and asks if I can give him a hand. In the barn we cut the twine on the bales and fork hay into the shed for bedding. I notice small droppings on the ground: rats or cats, I guess. T. has put some leftovers in a bowl for the cats on one of the bales. We line the trough in the shed with a blend of silage, beets, and vitamins from the mixer wagon. Then we go out to the field, where the cows respond to T.'s calls straight away, follow us into the shed, and tuck into the trough. We don't even have to touch them. Thang ya, says T. as he locks the gate. I think it's the first time he's thanked me. They ba'er come an elp muck out, he says.

Morning. My phone pings me awake like a command. I'm tired and need another hour's sleep, but check it anyway. An email from the company I bought my backpack from, telling me about new offers. Facebook telling me someone I met once years ago has updated her status. Google Maps couldn't find my location: PLEASE TURN ON LOCATION SERVICES. WhatsApp messages about a night out on a thread with a group of old friends from Norwich.

The day seeps through the curtains. S. is asleep. Now her phone beeps.

I get an automatic email with a job offer from an agency's online project management system; they call it a "community." Because of the time difference, the project managers will already be in their offices waiting for replies. I pick up my laptop from under the bed, log in, skim through the text as quickly as I can, and click to claim it before anyone else. I get it, with a deadline in the afternoon. I know I won't be able to fall asleep again; I knew it the minute I picked up the phone. But I'm too tired to get up properly. I click open the online translation program that's linked to the agency's site and look through the text. The program shows the text in two columns: on the left the original text, on the right a machine translation. Both columns are split into individual segments. I edit and save the first sentence of the machine translation, get stumped by the second, and click over to the American message board I spent an hour on before I fell asleep. After scrolling through memes, pictures, comments, and news, I realise all the posts are the same as the ones I looked at last night. I follow links to some news articles and a video of people falling over set to a techno soundtrack, which I quickly mute after S. groans and turns away. After an hour of this I put the computer back on the floor, get up, and go to the bathroom.

I willingly give my attention to those who compete to control it. As my attention shifts and flits, it turns into distraction. My attention and distraction become one and the same: a product. My boredom before it's dispersed in this way at least feels real: it weighs heavy on me and demands that I do something to lift it. When it drifts the way I let it, it's more akin to apathy, a thinning out of the mind that makes me uneasy. Why?

Outside dispersal, boredom and distraction have their places as parts of a whole. What looks like laziness can be part of meaningful work. You write something, get stuck, stare out the window or go for a walk, and suddenly the living truth that was there all along comes to you. In dispersal, by contrast, boredom becomes a kind of detachment that's very hard to turn to positive ends because it's unrooted in meaningful activity, meaningful time—because it's *controlled.*

Dispersal happens side by side with surveillance—at home, on the streets, at work. This country is a world leader in private and state CCTV cameras. If you call the police about a disturbance in a city, they'll often be able to see it happen in real time. Facial recognition cameras used for large-scale social control aren't far off. Every one of my clicks on the internet is tracked through my online and phone IDs and combined with detailed real-world data about me to create a digital double and build the most precise marketing profiles possible for *people like me*. My phone itself tries to connect to other devices to tailor the ads it will show me, even when I'm not using it. Algorithms guide me through the web, shaping my life in ways I don't understand.

As a freelancer in the countryside, I'm spared the apathy and unease of working in a physical office with pointless meetings, targets, performance reviews, competition, and monitoring by management. I have the privilege of time on my hands, of old-fashioned boredom; I'm free to say no to jobs. But being on the margins creates its own anxieties. I need to be contactable throughout the day. If I don't claim job offers straight away, some other freelancer, somewhere else in the world, will seize them first. I never know how many people a job has been offered to. I'm connected to the same networks as everyone else and if they're cut off I start to worry: what if it doesn't come back on? how will I pay the rent? what if we get evicted?

My time is largely structured around deadlines that I suspect the agencies make unnecessarily short to be more competitive themselves. I haven't raised my fees in ten years because of the likelihood of being undercut and improvements in machine translation, both of which enable agencies to pay translators less. It's a buyer's market, unfortunately, they tell me when I ask for more pay: supply exceeds demand. I work evenings, at weekends, on holidays. My monthly income varies wildly. I have no contracts, no financial safety net. From time to time an agency will stop sending me work—I never know why—and I have to send out another round of unsolicited emails to the addresses of potential clients I find online, or fill in new application forms on agency websites.

Fisher:

> Work and life become inseparable. Capital follows you when you dream. Time ceases to be linear, becomes chaotic, broken down into punctiform divisions. As production and distribution are restructured, so are nervous systems. To function effectively as a component of just-in-time production you must develop a capacity to respond to unforeseen events, you must learn to live in conditions of total instability.

For serious people, who live in the real world, there's only work and laziness. Boredom and anxiety are illusions, forms of laziness, and laziness is a moral failure to work, meaning to make money, even now when many have no prospects but debt and needless stress. You make your own prospects, you get out there and sell yourself, so that eventually you too can make money at other people's cost. That's just how it works, serious people will say.

In the early Christian church, *acedia* and *tristitia,* sloth and sadness, were deadly sins. They encompassed states such as boredom, laziness, and despair: sins of wilful withdrawal, flights from the divine. Unlike today, they were seen as problems of the whole person, to be cured not just through work but also through prayer and spiritual exercises: meaningful idleness. In prayer, endurance, and above all grace, the sufferer was meant to move from the darkness of self-enclosure into the light of God and the community of the faithful.

In their contemporary forms, these states are conditions to be overcome with drugs, cognitive behavioural therapy, and self-help techniques designed to empower sufferers to administrate themselves into fulfilment and re-enter the labour market with renewed vigour. But don't sloth and sadness still lie in wait among the workforce? And when they appear, don't they tell the truth about their everyday causes and the treatments we come up with?

Being ceaselessly lets things emerge, unfold, and reveal themselves, become what they are in relation to each other. It is a granting and a gathering. Our communication and surveillance networks are pale versions of it: operating within their own echoing worlds, mirroring vital forces and real human contact, they work not to let life thrive but to replace it with themselves. Within them being veils itself in us as all kinds of symptoms, regularly rebranded to sell us bogus cures.

We find big house spiders on the walls. I wipe away cobwebs every day. It's that time of year, says S. When she sees me about to kill one she stops me, cups it in her hands and brings it outside. I ask her the obvious question: won't they just come back in?

Drifts of dank leaves. Shuddering branches. The clocks go back and all of a sudden it's dark at five. In the mornings the bushes and hedges are cloaked in silvery webs. In T.'s garden the apples drop with precise thuds. I bring them to the pantry in a bucket along with a dozen pears which S. pickles in a brew of boiled vinegar, sugar, cloves, and cinnamon sticks. The kitchen windows steam up and the scent fills the house. I take a jar over to T.'s. The cows are moaning in the shed but he's not in there with them. I knock at the house, open the door and call, hear a sound from upstairs and go up. The wallpaper is peeling in two places and the stairs are stained with food. He's in bed.

What's wrong? I ask. You look pale.

I dun half feel queer, he says.

It's the left side of the belly, he says. I wonder aloud whether I should call an ambulance. Of course he says no. He'll be fine tomorrow, he says. He asks me to feed the cows for him. I go downstairs, put the kettle on, do the dishes, make a cup of tea, spoon some pears into a bowl. I try to make him drink and eat, but he tells me to leave the tea and the pears on the bedside table. I'll check on you tomorrow morning, I say. Call me if you feel worse.

I go to the shed and feed the cows.

Some months ago, one of the few small translation agencies I still work for was bought out by Denmark's biggest agency, which in turn was bought out by the biggest agency in the Nordic countries. Mass BCC'd emails were sent out about the great benefits and growth everyone could look forward to after these consolidations and synergies. Today I got an email from another freelancer saying they're shutting down the original agency, firing the staff and taking over their customers. The customers' money will flow out of the local area into the hands of a multinational. For freelancers, consolidations and synergies almost always mean more competition between one another, shorter deadlines, lower pay, and remoter management.

T. is up and about again. S. and I go to Morston to see the grey seals, which have started breeding on the Point formed of sand and shingle drifting up from the eroding eastern shore. The sky opens up beautifully when we reach the coast on the bus. Most of the passengers are looking at their phones.

Morston and its neighbouring village, Blakeney, used to be big seaports, but the harbours and river valley have silted up, in part due to the reclamation of the salt marshes, leaving room only for small boats. The seal tours are the main business now.

Quay sounds. Ropes creaking against poles, halyards clinking against masts, sea-spray spattering the staithe— a local word from the Norse for wharf. Our boatman, a retired lobster fisher, tells me he's seen the spit lengthen in his lifetime and the fishermen move to wider harbours to the west. The tides transform the coast here daily: the sea is drawn far out then surges back in, sometimes flooding the quay and the car park. At low tide you can walk all the way to the Point, where the seals feast on exposed sand eels.

Back on land, we walk to Stiffkey through green, brown, and grey saltmarshes broken up by pools and streams. The path is lined by tough, weather-beaten gorse with delicate yellow flowers. You can eat the flowers, says S., here, try. It tastes like coconut. Hundreds of stub-faced geese, newly arrived from the tundra, have gathered on the marshes to honk about who knows what.

We stop and look out over the spit through S.'s binoculars. Once you would have been able to walk here from Denmark. This coast was connected to the continent by a land mass, Doggerland, a rich habitat of wetland and wooded valleys navigated by nomadic hunter-gatherers who followed game and fish in seasonal patterns. If you'd stood on this spot with binoculars in that deep Mesolithic past, I imagine, you might have seen smoke from their fires here and there on the horizon. As temperatures rose and melted the northern glaciers, Doggerland flooded and Britain was cut off from mainland Europe. The people who were left on this island continued their nomadic way of life, burning scrubland and felling trees with flint tools to make temporary settlements, from which they tracked and hunted animals. In the Neolithic era they were displaced by migrants from the continent who brought wheat, barley, sheep, and goats, and who began to root themselves in the region, building enclosures and burial mounds. In the Bronze and Iron Ages, farming intensified. More forests were cleared by the Celts. Norfolk was settled by the Iceni, who surrendered to and then rebelled against the invading Romans. The collapse of the Roman Empire led to even more movement and migration: Germanic people from Anglia, on the shore of Jutland, arrived and built villages with open field systems, integrated with the Romanised Britons, and founded the kingdom of East Anglia. When the Danish Vikings invaded in the ninth century and themselves intermingled with the East Angles, they may have started digging for peat as they had done at home. Under Norman rule, Norfolk became the most populous and most farmed place in the country. It developed overseas trade links and later took in thousands of refugees from the Low Countries, the so-called Strangers, from whom many contemporary locals descend. By this time the rising sea had flooded the vast peat pits dug throughout the Middle Ages and was slowly shaping the landscape that became known as the Broads.

Years ago, when I first started exploring the Norfolk countryside, I recognised many of the village names. The county is dotted with Danish place names from the time of the Danelaw, many mixed with Old English words. They made me feel less of a stranger. But whose home is this in any case? Flora, fauna, history, and geology: all seem as provisional here as the shifting sands of the coast itself.

As provisional as these words, which slip and shift from under me. The day remains what it is, stretching out, silent. I'm a babble of voices, both inside and outside the day. Odd predicament. Then find words that can take hold in you. Speak for yourself and see the world as if awakening. Words are alive, they can resist dead time. They're not entirely drained of meaning, not entirely dedicated to capital—not yet. The word's not the thing, the thing not the word, but when the right word for the thing is found, the thing emerges. All happen at once: word, world, speaker. The distant day now suddenly close.

I watch the spider work under the eave outside the window, sheltered from the wind and rain. What does it show me, in its patience? It spins its filaments out of itself, arranges and rearranges them. One thread quivers and drops off the eave: the spider crawls up to replace it, stops to rest, starts again. Slim pickings in this weather, but what else can it do but build its net, mend it when it breaks, rebuild elsewhere when its weaving is disturbed, and wait? It's so easily displaced, and so easily makes another home. Each unique web spreads out in any old nook, its gaps growing wider, sometimes visible only in sunlight. The worker sits still for an age, its labours apparently all for nothing, until the web is either wiped away (as I'll probably wipe away this one when the weather's dry) or comes into its own when shaken to life by an insect. The spider can't control when the insect will come; perhaps it never will.

We, by contrast, cast our fine-meshed nets over the Earth, mapping and monitoring it with pinpoint accuracy. Military-developed GPS satellites circle the globe, linking to billions of receivers on the ground, synchronising them via atomic clocks. They plot every millimetre of the planet, guiding missiles and aiding logistics, stock market trading, weather forecasts, infrastructure grids, the internet. Even farming machines are now fitted with positioning systems that automate ploughing, planting, and harvesting. The modern farmer can run his driverless tractors from his home office while he looks up weather reports and sells his grain on the global market.

A dark age that insists on closing all gaps in the world, leaving nothing to chance. But the more we cover it up, the more nature hides from us, leaving us to our own devices.

My mobile pings. I check it in the kitchen, the bathroom, the pub, wherever I know there's a signal. I *want* it to ping. I feel bereft when it doesn't.

I get a message from T.'s sister saying that T.'s in hospital. At the same time I get an email marked URGENT about a translation I sent yesterday: the customer has criticisms and extra text she wants translated before she gives her presentation this afternoon. I reply to T.'s sister, saying I'll come as soon as I can. I have trouble opening the customer's document because PowerPoint needs to be updated and I have to reset the router because the connection cuts out. Finally I send the email with the revised file attached and hope that's the end of it.

I've missed the bus, so I have to bike to the hospital. When I arrive, sweaty, I'm led to T.'s bed, where he's hooked up to wires and drips. It's the pancreas, he says. Cancer.

They need to do more tests but it doesn't look good. He says he got a call last month from a property developer who wants to buy the farm and now he's considering the offer. I'm not sure what to say.

There ent much to say is there? he says.

What does he want to do with the place? I ask.

Make it into something posh I imagine, he says, like all the rest of em.

He gives me his house keys and asks me to turn on the heating in the evening if it gets frosty so the pipes don't freeze. I say I'll come back soon and tell him to call me if he needs anything. He nods and I leave, feeling guilty.

I got drunk on the way back from the hospital and dropped my laptop on the street between pubs. It wouldn't turn on. The next day I bought a new one from Amazon. When it arrived the following week and I tried to set it up, it was very slow. I spent two days sorting out email, internet, Office, deleting colourful, bouncing tiles, and turning off the automatic services. It took half a day to install thirty per cent of an Office update. I lost work and started to get seriously worried. I didn't know what to do. Find another job? I supposed I could go round the farms and ask if anyone needed help. I finally understood my mistake after looking it up on S.'s laptop, which was also lagging. I'd put in our wifi password during the Windows setup process instead of clicking SKIP, which caused all the bloatware to start up and slow everything to the point where I could hardly use the new machine: it was bogging itself down with its own pre-installed advertising and monitoring programs, while at the same time linking up to our other devices and slowing them down too.

When we can, we help T.'s helpers with the cows and chickens and picking up the deliveries. We still get some customers knocking for fruit, vegetables, and eggs. I put the money in a drawer in T.'s kitchen.

We visit him. His face is sallow. He asks S. to plug in his phone charger. He's too weak, this big strong man with a lifetime of physical labour behind him. He says he's accepted the developer's offer, and the man will bring the contract tomorrow for him to sign. Jesus, I say, don't you want to have someone look it over? What's the rush? He looks me in the eye until I have to look down. They ent even gonna operate, he says. S. takes his hand. We sit in silence. When ya gotta gew, ya gotta gew, he says finally. On the way out we speak to a doctor who tells us the biopsy showed that the cancer has already spread to the liver and it looks like the best thing for T. is a bed in the hospice.

More business texts. I must have translated thousands over the years. The ones that describe corporate philosophies tend to say the same things. They talk about creativity, innovation, ideas, relationships, navigating a dynamic world, having the courage to face challenges through openness to change, and so on. They, and I along with them, often describe their business, products, and employees as if they were all part of a vital existential journey, fraught with trials but moving towards ever-greater success. They're always moving forward, always positive.

I suddenly start crying while doing the dishes. What the hell difference is that going to make, I say to myself as I wash my face.

En ulykke kommer sjældent alene, goes a Danish saying: misfortunes rarely come alone. I installed an adblocker app on my phone that must have been malware, because the whole device started slowing down, finally crashed, and won't turn back on. Now I itch to check it. I look for it on my bedside table when I wake up in the morning, reach for it in my coat pocket on my walks. I take the bus to Norwich to get it fixed. I go back to the place where I bought it. The assistant tries to turn it on and confirms it's broken. Since it's out of warranty, fixing it is apparently a huge undertaking that requires sending it away to technicians, who'll need to check whether the problem is a software issue, a motherboard malfunction, or something else. Often the handset has been dropped or there's been spillage, the assistant says. I tell him I haven't dropped it or spilled anything on it. Often people do that without knowing it, he says. It might be that or it might be something else, he adds. Either way the cost could run up and it probably won't be worth it; you'd be better off buying a new one. He shows me lots of different pricing and insurance packages. I end up too confused to make a decision, tell him I'm sorry but I have to be somewhere, and leave while he's still talking. I go to the manufacturer's outlet, where an assistant turns it back on in an instant and shows me how to do a factory reset. I tell her I installed an adblocker that may have made it crash. She asks me if it was free and I say it was. She shakes her head and says, Nothing good comes for free these days.

We visit T. in the hospice. He's sunk into a haze of pain. He knows it's us but we can't reach him. He shifts and moans; the bed creaks under his weight. S. puts some of her balm on his cracked lips. I don't know how to feel. I can't stop looking at the sleep in the corners of his eyes.

His phone is on the floor, charging, showing unread messages.

We help T.'s sister clean and tidy his house. She's brusque, loud, and efficient. I tell her about the money in the drawer. She opens it, puts the notes in her bra, and gives me the change in a plastic bag. This is pointless, really, she says in an Essex accent as we clean, cos the clearance men will just track mud all over the place, but it just seems like the right thing to do. I'm about to snap something back about that being a bit premature when I realise she's right. She straightens up and her face softens. She looks at me and says: It's all happened so fast, innit?

The phone reset did away with all my social media apps. When I tell S. I might try just to use my phone for emails from now on, she says she's installed an app on hers that can block other apps such as internet browsers—that protects you from yourself. She shows me how it works. Why didn't you tell me about this before? I ask. I did, she says. You must not have been listening. You were probably on your phone.

It's too cold and rainy to run and cycle outside, but S. has found some YouTube fitness videos you can do at home using your own bodyweight. We move the furniture against the walls. It feels silly at first but is surprisingly tough. Rookie ran away when we first started, but he's used to it now. He watches us warily from a distance.

Bleak fields. Branches glistening with hoar frost on the way down to the river. I think of Wallace Stevens' mind of winter. Does that help? I can't decide, it's too cold to think. A boat chugs by, leaving a dense wobbling wake in the near-freezing water. The path is ridged with hard mud. On the surface of the willow pond, the freshwater forms shapes that look like oil slicks as the brackish water sinks and starts to freeze. I spot a snipe at the edge of the pond, blended into the reeds and puffed up against the cold, its long beak sticking out from under its wing. Everything here seems indrawn and dormant: waiting, conserving energy, secretly growing. On the way back, black ice slicks the road and frost feathers on car windshields spread out in unique, intricate patterns.

I toy with the idea of deleting my Facebook account, which I haven't logged into for months anyway. Then I would be truly cut off out here—from real people who've been part of my life, for good and bad; from friends, acquaintances, relatives. Yet all these years it's been tracking me across the internet via its icon to sell ads through real-time auctions, and still is, even though I'm not logged in. All these years, reducing me and my friends to saleable data points, filtering our feeds, guiding our eyes to what's most valuable to its interests.

To wean yourself off your skewed allegiances. To work yourself through your fear of missing out and your need for acceptance, the empty pleasures of instant communicability, in whatever way is best for you. Futile gestures, maybe, but what if enough people did it to reach negative critical mass: simply refused?

Isn't that why I came out here, to get time and space to think?

A., a friend of S.'s from Cambridge, comes to visit for the weekend and we take a walk together. He's a real birder, the kind of English naturalist I can't help but think of, perhaps unfairly, as continuing the Victorian tradition of cataloguing and comprehending every part of the Earth. He talks like many young men do, loudly and as if he's indisputably right. On our walks he spots straight away what's going on in the environment. He can name and explain anything you ask about, or knows someone who's writing a thesis about it. Binoculars in hand, he sees a sparrowhawk and bearded tits, which we can't see even when he points them out to us. He hears fieldfares and redwings and tells us all about their breeding and migration patterns and how they're changing because of global warming. What was that? I ask, seeing something brown flash by like an arrow. That was just a wren, he says, looking for more interesting finds. For me, though I like hearing about them, the smaller birds and their songs tend to fade into the general ambience of the place: they rustle and call to each other, flit in the backdrop, but are never *quite* there. But, for A., who regularly rings and tags birds, they have definite individual presences, even if only as representatives of their species. He can tell the females from the males, the juveniles from the adults; he can detect seasonal changes in their plumage, behaviour, and calls. He can collate, analyse, and extrapolate from his data, using it to predict future outcomes and demonstrate trends in the wider environment. I get the impression that he sees all the other parts of the landscape in the same way: each can be understood in terms of its place and function in the habitat, each habitat within the larger ecosystem, and so on in widening circles. I can only ask him so much on our way through the woods and along the river before I start to feel like an irrelevant part of the landscape, and irrelevant even to him. Over dinner he keeps talking and doesn't ask us any questions. When he leaves the next morning, we feel as if a weight has lifted.

A leaflet about recycling and fly-tipping reminds me of the kayak I abandoned in the summer. Now that the water is freezing, it might be possible to retrieve it. In the afternoon I put my wellies on and go down to the river, and manage to find both the kayak and the seat. I drag them out of the brush, up to the road. I have to pass by N.'s place on the way home, so I drop in, and over a mug of tea in his cluttered kitchen I tell him what happened. He says he'll pick up the kayak in his van later on. Either he'll fix it or take it to the tip.

Not being able to browse the internet on my phone is a relief. I don't carry it with me everywhere. Sometimes I even forget about it. I take it with me on my way to the shops in case S. texts me about something we need, but I don't pull it out of my pocket as often.

Today I stopped at an ash tree and looked at the buds on its branches: slick black growths dense with life in the middle of winter. I looked at them until I realised how cold I was. I jumped and shook myself warm. No, this isn't a season of death, I thought on my way home to the cottage. Those buds point back and forth between the seasons, just as each season points back and forth to the others. Isn't nature always at home in itself?

For us, I think, home must have something to do with questioning, since it's not given to us as it is to plants and animals. But sometimes what's sought guides the search: the answer is in the question. What am I but my questions put to work in me, to open me up to what's already open to me?

To a young man seeking guidance from him, Rilke wrote:

> Be patient with everything that's unresolved in your heart and try to love the questions themselves as if they were locked rooms or books written in a foreign language. Don't look for answers that can't be given to you now... Live the questions now. Maybe then, one day in the far-off future, you will find that—little by little, without noticing it—you have lived your way into the answer.

Lorries with huge trailers have taken the cows and chickens from T.'s farm. They had to move quickly, I guess. Who knows where they've gone? The lorries scared off the birds for a while and left deep ruts in the path. The neighbouring farmer knocks on the door and tells us he's been to see T. and that we can have the eggs and do whatever we want with the fruit and vegetable patches. It's all gun be tore up anyway, he says. Just as well thas winter.

Dogwalkers everywhere. In town, on the paths, on the coast. I've trained myself to ignore dogs when they come up to me. I used to pet them and speak to their owners, a habit I got from my father's side of the family. My mother's side were all farmers, unsentimental about animals.

Through many centuries of domestication, dogs have evolved special eyebrow muscles that make them more appealing to humans and allow them to adopt that pleading look people find so cute. I stopped fussing over them when I learned this. I even leave Rookie alone most of the time now (S. spoils him).

First snowfall of the year. The birds leave rune-like marks on the lawn as they peck at the bread crusts we throw out for them. S. hung a ball of suet for them next to N.'s rook the other day, but it's gone now. A squirrel must have stolen it.

Today I went to the hospice to see T. and was told he'd died this morning. I called his sister. She said she's arranging the funeral. I went to turn his heating on. I sat looking at the floor for a while in my coat and hat, then turned the heating off and went home.

Sunday. S. is taking a full day off work, her first in a long time. She lies in bed drinking tea, eating crisps, and watching an American sitcom. She says she feels sad and rundown. You need a blast of sea air, I say, and make her get dressed, though I feel the same. Again the sky seems to clear when we reach the coast. We walk on stones sucked smooth by the tides, the sea-sides of our faces numbed by the wind. Gulls quarrel over something on the shoreline. There are patches of cracked ice on the heavy wet sand and grasses growing out of the cliff. I love the part of the beach where the cliff turns inland and the sea seems to open up. On the horizon are the revolving white blades of wind turbines built by a Danish company I translate for. We turn back and drink ales by the fireplace in a pub while waiting for the bus, and get ruddy and lightheaded. The funeral is next Saturday.

I left my phone at home and didn't check it until a couple of hours after we returned. There were no emails anyway. I realise I don't miss social media at all, perhaps because hardly any of what happens there is meaningful in the first place. It creates a feedback loop of self-doubt and desire for approval that you only crave while you're inside it. Delete the loop and it vanishes like the mirage it was.

It seems to me that most of us knew this instinctively in the early days of the internet, when it was embarrassing to admit to being on social media, to have found a partner on a dating site, and so on, but we forgot it as the virtual became normalised.

The social media designers and bosses, those hijackers of the mind, know the effects of what they've engineered better than anyone. In fact many of them use their own platforms less than you'd think, and many won't let their children use them.

Sean Parker, Facebook's founding president:

> God only knows what it's doing to our children's brains... The thought process was, how do we consume as much of your time and conscious attention as possible? It's exactly the kind of thing that a hacker like myself would come up with, because you're exploiting a vulnerability in human psychology... The inventors, creators, understood this consciously. And we did it anyway.

More storms. Leaves fly off the trees like birds. Near the shops a huge oak has fallen across the road, its trunk peeled open, a shock of white against the drab surroundings.

The funeral is in the parish church on a damp grey afternoon. As we walk to a pew, we nod to some locals we know from the pub and the shops, the neighbouring farmer and his workers, T.'s sister and a couple of suppliers. Annoyingly formal, unnatural movements. My suit smells musty. While S. dabs her eyes with a tissue I'm distracted by a puddle forming under an umbrella, the wheels of a walker turning different ways, steam rising from an electric heater... Nothing genuine in me, just an awkward, self-conscious sadness.

The paths along the river are flooded and trees have fallen over in the woods. Tree surgeons have already gone to work on some them. I pass a wall of orange discs: the ends of neatly stacked alder logs.

S. has left her iPad on the sofa. On a whim I pick it up and log into Facebook to check my messages. There's only one, from a friend asking if I'm coming to the party she posted an invite for and whether I'm still living in *the arse end of nowhere*. When I try to reply, a window pops up instructing me to install the Messenger app. I refresh the page, try again, and the same thing happens. That's enough, I think. I refresh again, click SETTINGS and look for a DELETE ACCOUNT button. There isn't one, of course. I close the window and my eyes are immediately drawn down the page full of status updates, pictures, and comments by people I used to know. I catch myself, scroll back up, and find the HELP search bar, type in *delete account*, and am taken to a window where I can submit my account for deletion within fourteen days. I click the button.

Who knows whether they'll erase all the data they've collected on me through my likes, my messages, the posts and pictures that other people tagged me in. No doubt it's already out there, being farmed by marketing companies. I search for what happens to your data after you cancel your account and click on a link to a forum where someone has asked the same question, but the page is blocked by a sign-in window that requires me to validate my identity through Google—or Facebook. I turn off the iPad and put it away with a rare sense of finality.

Finally: a sunny day. I run around the football fields at the school and do pull-ups on the crossbars. Snowdrops have come up under the trees. A dog—a stray?—runs up and sniffs at me, then runs away. I remember the cats on the farm. They must be starving. When I get back I bring a bowl of Rookie's food and a tupperware container to the haybarn. I leave the bowl on the bale where I saw T. had put out leftovers, and fill the container with water from the tap in the cowshed. I look around for droppings but don't see any. The next day I find the bowl licked clean.

S. tells me people on our WhatsApp groups have been wondering why I left. One asked her if I was angry about something, another if I'd *finally cracked out there lol*. I resist the urge to look at the exchanges on S.'s phone. M. texts me and asks if I'm all right, and a former Facebook friend emails to say: *Thanks for unfriending me, dickhead.*

I go to Norwich to buy new clothes. While I'm there I go to my mobile network provider's shop to ask if they can reduce my rate, since I'm not using the phone as much these days. The assistant tells me I need to call customer service. But I'm in the shop, I say. I know, he says, I'm sorry but we don't deal with that, we just do sales. I leave the shop, go to a pub and call customer service. I'm given six options, then four other options, then transferred to three different members of staff in an Indian call centre. I have to explain my situation and give my number, my name, and three letters of my password to each person. I end up in the sales department. When I ask to have my bill reduced the assistant keeps interrupting me with other offers. I hang up, wondering how they feel about what they're made to do.

I wake up wrong. The day's all wrong: a series of separate moments that don't fit. S. is in a bad mood, too. We move around awkwardly, each of us irritated by the sounds the other makes, the propaganda on the radio, Rookie's pestering for food. Even the fitful wind seems irritated. I move from the bed to the living room with my laptop, then back to the bed when S. starts playing a podcast in the kitchen. Finally I shove away the laptop and go and make it up with S. We hug, prepare lunch together, and start joking again. It was nothing, we agree, some days just don't get off the ground.

K., who works with S., comes up from Norwich and drives us to Southwold on the Suffolk coast. We eat dinner in a pub and walk down the damp pier. The yellow beam from the lighthouse sweeps through the fog, over the black water, the houses along the road, the mural of George Orwell, who lived and wrote here.

The beam lends an eerie greenish hue to everything it passes over. It's like the last scene of a film, says K., where there's a battle, a couple have to part or someone swims ashore from a shipwreck. We amuse ourselves by making up increasingly absurd scenarios for movie endings, probably to relieve the oppressive atmosphere of the place. Except it's not oppressive, is it, I think to myself as we walk back to the car, or a set for anything, tragic or comic. It's nothing but itself. A cold dark coast, neither benign nor hostile.

Only one real question, however kitschy it sounds: how to live in the face of the impersonal. Not to cover it up with your own stories but to accept it with your whole being and try to find joy in it. Orwell described the nightmare of a world controlled by a single story, where every person, every act and thought must conform to a certain end. We appear to live in a freer world, a world of infinite stories, where everyone can make up their own. But within this multiplicity we too are guided and controlled, pressed to conform to taken-for-granted ends, submit to our age's imperatives of success and self-fashioning. In our world, too, fewer and fewer chinks are left open in the armour of the everyday for the impersonal to show us the smallness of our own stories and the true horizon of our possibilities.

Monday morning. I wait for work, but there's nothing. I consider sending out some unsolicited applications, then decide to take the train to Wroxham and go for a walk. Passing through the station in the past, I noticed a promising sign saying THE HEART OF THE BROADS with a map and some images of local wildlife. Drab, dun landscape under the huge, ever-changing Norfolk sky. One moment, snow flurries blur the treelines. The next, distant clouds separate and corridors of light pour down on stubby fields and grey lots. A path by the station leads to a riverside boardwalk, which turns out to be very short. As I walk back and head for the village shops, three jobs pop up on my phone. I find a pub, order half a pint, and ask for the wifi password. I sit down, pull out my laptop, and check the agency's site. The texts have been taken. I finish my drink, go to one of the boat hire places and ask whether there are any footpaths nearby. The woman behind the counter points to a map of the river and tells me, It's all private land round here, there's nowhere to walk, but you can rent one of our boats. I thank her and go back in the other direction, thinking there must be *somewhere*. There's nature all around! I walk for an hour along a road between large farmers' fields, snow tickling my face, cars and lorries thundering past. The usual crows and pigeons.

I eat a sloe berry from a hedge that's survived the winter and my mouth dries up. I stop to get a bottle of water out of my backpack and a car sprays my legs as it drives through a puddle. I check my phone: another job. I realise I'm getting nowhere and go back to the station. When I get home I check the agency's site again to see whether the job's been claimed. It has.

In the still, snowy evening, we walk to the pub for dinner. All sounds are muffled. In the British tradition the small roads haven't been cleared, and there are no cars, so we walk where we want on sheets of compacted snow gleaming under the full moon. Tonight we don't need our torches. After the meal I go outside to smoke. Under the pub's yellow light, the shadows of the snowflakes look like swarms of insects.

Blanketed earth, leaden sky. What lifts the heaviness? A beautiful line in a book. One of S.'s weird jokes. A flash of sunlight. Rookie waking up and running around the room for no reason... Give us this day our daily bread, says the prayer: give us our manna from heaven, the fullness of time, not just this day but every day, every moment.

There's some truth to Pascal's saying that all human miseries stem from one's inability to sit quietly in a room alone. *If man were happy,* he wrote, *the less he were diverted the happier he would be, like the saints and God.* Kafka said evil is what distracts, and fantasised about living in a cell buried deep in the earth in which he could do nothing but write: he'd be passed food through a slot. Monks of certain orders are said to have slept in their coffins... Give me a break. If I don't get a good long dose of sunshine soon, I'll start dribbling. I bring up the possibility of a holiday to S. again. She's working on ancient Anatolia and says she'd like to see Istanbul. I say I'd prefer not to go to a big city and we leave it there. While we think about it, we work, do the laundry, eat, and the sun comes out, the snow melts, the eaves drip, and the branches shine. Spring seems as if it's really happening and a holiday seems less urgent.

Two days later another cold front hits us and the weather's Siberian again. S. goes out to the garden with scissors, cuts the daffodils that froze as they started to bloom, and puts them in a vase in the kitchen. By late afternoon they've thawed and come back to life in the sunlight. I can smell their scent from the living room.

In the morning a removals lorry drives up to the farm. I wonder if T.'s sister is over there. I have a deadline, so I don't leave the cottage to check. In the afternoon the lorry comes back down. I go out to feed T.'s cats while S. cooks dinner. The cowshed smells sickly sweet of manure and rotting hay, so I scrape it all into the pit under the shed and rinse the floor with the power washer. I let myself into T.'s house. His sister was right: there's dried mud and leaves on the floor. How still it all seems, how abandoned already.

N. calls to tell me to come and see the sculpture he's made from my old bike and other scrap metal, forged or melted down and recast. He's kept it quiet. He says he might have ruined it if he'd talked about it. I had no idea he was capable of something like this. It's a tree, about seven feet tall and so elaborate I have to walk around it for a while to take it in. The trunk is made of thick, twisted ropes of grey and black wrought iron, with delicate ridges and knots. The branches and crown are an intricate network of matte and brushed metals, some with faded colours, some with parts of trademarks still on. The leaves are paper-thin sheets of tin and copper with veins and teeth. The more I look, the more I see. There's a burr on the trunk made from part of a curled-up bike chain— mine, presumably. Here and there are streaks of hard polished wood. There's a bag made of brass with a Tesco label somehow embossed on it, wrinkled and draped across the branches with incredible precision. N. starts telling me all about how he made it, but I say I don't want to know the details: I want to know it only in this form, as if I'd come across it in some apocalyptic landscape. Someone might eventually, he says, it'll last forever. It better. I burnt myself like ten times. Call it *End-Times Tree*, I suggest. You can probably sell it for much more than I can afford. He says he'll try Lord Whatever of Holkham Hall: maybe he'll want it for the park. That seems unlikely, I think to myself. Or someone might want it in their second garden up there, he says, there's an arts and crafts fair soon in Holt. He says he doesn't bother with what he calls the pastel tearoom galleries anymore. I can tell they're getting ready to say no as soon as they see me, he says. I take pictures of the tree with my phone and tell him I might be able to help.

This is what it all led up to, he says as he walks around it. Three years it took, with lots of do-overs. I won't top it, I can feel it. And that's fine. But it's gonna be weird if I manage to sell it; I'd prefer to keep it here so I can look at it now and then and show my friends, instead of some stranger owning it. Like, actually *owning* it.

Long rainy days indoors. Winter isn't ready to loosen its grip. Work has dwindled. I haven't heard from one of my main sources of income for the better part of a month.

I feel the old heaviness sink over me again, the sense of worthlessness. As always I don't know how much of it is my own doing—whether I've done something to cause it or haven't done enough to prevent it. I need a break, I tell S., let's go somewhere, where can we go? She says she'll think about it, but this weekend she has to go to London for a meeting.

I email the photos of N.'s tree to myself and set up profiles for him on a couple of art market websites. I call him and ask him what he'd want to charge while I scroll through the prices of other sculptures. We agree on a price at the high end. I email G., who I used to drink with in Norwich. He lectures at the arts college and works as an arts coordinator for the council. I attach the pictures, tell him there's a sculptor out here he should visit, and ask if he still has his gallery contacts. He'll almost certainly be too busy to reply.

Friday. S. has gone. To write yourself out of a bad mood. Now I have time, nothing but time, but nothing to say. I had hoped a job would be posted today just so I'd have something to do over the weekend. I heard a beep while I was in the bathroom, but the text had already been claimed by the time I returned to my computer.

Lift yourself out of it. Clean the house. No, too much work. Go for a walk. No, too dull. Do it anyway.

After dinner I take a sleeping pill, find a Danish crime series to watch on a streaming site, and smoke a cigarette in the garden while I wait for the first episode to load. When I come back, the screen's blocked by weight-loss and penis-enlargement ads.

The next day I visit N. with my backpack full of beer. We sit in his barn and drink. I look at his sculpture and watch him tinker with his things. Then I go home, eat, and sleep for an hour. When I wake, it takes me a while to figure out what time it is.

Hard to keep this journal these days. My thoughts, when I have them, are slow and ponderous, like something heavy moving in water. I grab small jobs here and there, check the headlines, stare out the window, read an extract from a novel on the internet, watch YouTube videos, get restless, get hungry. It's not enough, this fractional way of life, this waste of time. It can take an hour to focus my thoughts, even when S. is away.

Yet another cold turn, just as the leaves and flowers were coming out. Things seem to shrink back from the cutting wind. It's as if the season itself is confused. There's a shaft of ice under the drainpipe at the corner of the cottage. I hit it with a hammer while holding the pipe in place. Another shaft drops out: I hit each one until the ice is gone and a trickle of water runs out.

Many days without an entry here. We've both had the flu. S. must have brought it back from London. But I was quick enough at least to claim a big job—a tech company's staff policy—which saved my month and which I translated in bed, probably badly. Looking over this journal I barely recall the upbeat mood of some passages. But today the first scents of spring have brought a throb of life. The work of the new season is starting and the trees are budding. It feels almost impossible after a winter in which nothing seemed able to begin.

There are land surveyors in high-vis vests on T.'s farm, moving tripods about and measuring the plot with GPS equipment.

N. texts to say he's sold his tree for slightly less than the asking price after a posh man from Suffolk who saw it online rang and came to visit him. (G. never replied.) He says it's saved his year: he was broke and living on baked beans, tea, and reduced Co-op sandwiches. He even looked for roadkill to bring home when he was driving. I never knew. I wish I'd brought him more eggs and vegetables.

Tree surgeons and reed-cutters are making room for new growth, opening up the landscape. The birds, flushed out of their hiding places, are everywhere. Pheasants flap and squall in the brush at the end of the field. In the garden a pair of magpies are madly nest-building. In the woods, green shoots are growing through blankets of dead leaves and bracken. The hedges along the road are flowering and S. says she spotted her first bumblebee yesterday. By the river we see a blue tit hacking open a bulrush and spitting downy wisps to all sides. What's it after, we wonder: nest bedding? seeds? insects? We move close but it's too busy to care about us. Today I feel no need to leave this place.

Spring is here in the nearest things, in the smell of the grass and weeds and the air, as the Earth lavishly renews itself.

In everything well-known something worthy of thought still lurks, wrote Heidegger. Something can take hold. There are crocuses among the empty lager cans and crisp packets on the patch of grass beside the Co-op. There are primroses under the bare fig tree in the cemetery.

Writing about conservation, the Norfolk-based naturalist Mark Cocker says it's the commonplace that should be protected, not the rare:

> Our inherent orientation towards the rare has often distorted the way in which we look at the environment. How often one finds conservation policies built around a few charismatic species, such as the tiger, polar bear or, more parochially, the Eurasian bittern or corncrake. Singling out the flagship animal is often a way of simplifying a project for public consumption... when what truly makes an ecosystem flourish is the very opposite of its flagship representative: the sheer bio-luxuriance of its commonest constituents.

Moreover, he says, *a preoccupation with the exceptional is almost hardwired into the human imagination.* As with flagship nature programmes, it's increasingly difficult to escape the lure of the exceptional and marketable over what's right in front of us. The familiar is harder to appreciate.

I move between the bedroom and bathroom, the study and living room, the cottage and the Co-op, day in, day out. I grow too used to the world again. I make it too familiar, let the moment veil itself in the everyday. I become a burden to myself.

Sometimes the nearest things are the hardest to see. We see them too often to see them fresh, and understandably seek to escape them when they seem to have lost all mystery, all *presence*. Too much home and home becomes opaque, flat. I'm a body walking through the same rooms and fields and shops. No mountain peaks on this plain, no vantage point. The same, the same. The impulse is to look for a quick escape into the new and exciting, or a slow escape into resignation and resentment.

But doesn't the commonplace hold its own secrets? Perhaps only our impatience obscures them. If we had the endurance of animals we might be better able to accept the familiar and simply wait, day after undistinguished day, until the day, unmasked, surrendered.

Doesn't being lurk most mysteriously—nearest and furthest—among the things we move around every day, in the fact of their being here at all? Now on my walks I sometimes stop and look at one thing for as long as I can, a squirrel, say, or a flowering bush, until I see its strangeness again, the essential strangeness of its being, to which I'm somehow linked.

For my father, who travelled the world as a diplomat and took us with him to different countries, everything was familiar. He received his orders from the Ministry of Foreign Affairs back home, followed them to the letter, and was praised by his superiors. This gave him a vantage point from which he could grasp whatever he encountered. If new information appeared that contradicted something he said, it didn't matter, since it was all encompassed within the same horizon. Nothing seemed to surprise him. Everything had happened before in some form or another, and if it hadn't, it would barely make a dent in the general order of things anyway: *plus ça change*, history repeats itself, the poor will always be with us. He read books about statecraft, biographies of statesmen. He was an Anglophile, but a lover of an outmoded image of Britain: he admired easygoing landowners in costume dramas who knew everyone's place and dismissed their servants' trivial complaints with a lordly wave of the hand. His favourite saying was *the exception that proves the rule*, and the rule could be as general as he liked, could absorb any event or emotion, could be made to span human history and life itself. In this way he swept his arm across the horizon and familiarised himself with the world.

By contrast, when I went to university everything seemed to be about the exception rather than the rule. We were to learn the practice of *theory*, which in those days mainly involved focusing on marginal subjects: the edges of traditional academic disciplines and canons, of history and language, even of thought itself. It was the focus on the marginal that was thought to give theory its subversive force.

We learned, first, that meaning was endlessly constructed and deferred along fluid chains of signs, and that any statement about general rules had to be put in scare quotes and examined for its underlying, historically contingent biases. We learned to be suspicious of *the natural*. We read texts by airy French philosophers we pretended to understand. We made ironic comments about earnest, outmoded writers to show each other we'd seen through and moved past that kind of thing. We wrote and talked about neglected artists, writers, and thinkers, about ruptures, about the abject and the liminal, and so on. It was thrilling to use this new language. We were deconstructing all oppressive essentialisms, even the notion of the stable subject itself, the ability to say "I"!

I absorbed the unwritten rules of theory easily since there was nothing very solid in me to resist them. I made sure to use the latest buzzwords and subject my own arguments to the same suspicion I directed at my subject matter, to the point where I wasn't saying anything meaningful at all. By the end, I remember, I saw writing essays as more of an aesthetic exercise than an intellectual one. I got almost cynical. I did what I needed to get good grades.

By constantly re-examining the conditions and limits of thought, theory seemed to lose its own critical force. In the end it didn't have much more to offer than revisions of the jargon of the marginal and sceptical interrogations of texts that dared to take standpoints and express real emotions. By substituting the *forms* of thought for any sustaining *content* of thought (and what could that possibly mean for us?) our studies were preparing us perfectly for what was already happening in the "real" world— where the flow of capital was at work erasing the borders between the centre and the margins without our help, bringing the outside in and the inside out. Our minds were being prepared for what we'd soon be thrown into. In the real world, the exceptional could no longer be used effectively to break down anything; everything was already breaking down. Entrepreneurs were putting their best people on capturing the exceptional in every possible way, from using alternative music and avant-garde art in ads to tapping into minority markets. Exceptions were being absorbed into the norm and the norm was to become absorbed into the new order of things: precarity.

So, in a sense, my father's *laissez-faire* attitude had now become fitting for these times in ways he probably couldn't have imagined: the general rule swallows all exceptions, nothing you do will make much difference, the poor will always be with us.

The blackthorns and fruit trees are blossoming, forget-me-nots have replaced the crocuses and primroses, and the trees are leafing. Budbursts everywhere! It's sunny and our open windows let in frantic flies and bees, a white butterfly. S. is weeding. She comes in smelling of fresh air and earth.

We take out the foraging book again. We pick nettles, wild garlic, and dandelions, and look up recipes for them.

Yesterday an excavator rumbled up the path and started demolishing T.'s farm. We had to close the windows because of the noise and dust. I went outside and watched from the edge of the courtyard. The cowshed was already a heap of rubble. I worried about the cats and bats. Weeds and hollyhocks had grown to the windows of the house, which the excavator was hacking into like a giant steel bird. A man stood in the courtyard with T.'s power washer, aiming a jet of water at the holes the machine made in the roof. A Range Rover rolled up and a tall young man wearing a gilet got out and looked around. He came over to me, introduced himself as the developer, and stood there as if waiting for me to explain my presence. Then his mobile rang and he walked off to take the call. A minute later he came back, and as we watched the demolition he said, by way of small talk, Small farms have to diversify or die these days I'm afraid. He was still angling for the reason I was there. I didn't take the bait. Did you know the owner? he asked. Yes, I said, and walked away.

In the woods a tree lies chopped up where it fell, as if it's been dissected. I hope the tree surgeons forget about it so I can watch it slowly be claimed by insects, mushrooms, and moss.

A sleepless night. The huge night and the slow dawn. The sound of the binmen tipping our tins and bottles into their lorry, interrupting the birdcalls. The same old sense of final emptiness, which makes the thoughts I formulate in the day in front of my computer, with my grown-up books around me, seem contrived and forced onto something almost helpless—onto what Gombrowicz called *a furtive childhood, a concealed degradation.* Completely unacceptable, I think, like the wronged consumer I am: why should anyone be made to deal with this, day after day?

There's something to it, I tell myself, the old idea that despair is a seductive sin, a sickness unto death. That's one thing the Christians always understood, that there are feelings we indulge at our own risk. But when the feeling is this long-lived, this unshakeable?

In the afternoon I got caught in a thunderstorm biking back from the shops and cursed this backwoods village while getting splattered with mud. Of course the downpour stopped just as I arrived home. I peeled off all my clothes and put them in the washing machine, rummaged for washing powder under the sink, realised we'd run out, and stormed to the bathroom in a childish rage. S.

asked me something but I didn't answer. When I'd showered and calmed down I asked her what she said. She said she asked me what I wanted for dinner.

A long dream last night. I was in a car, being driven somewhere. Outside, souped-up roadsters with young men behind the wheels started ramming each other to get across a bridge. I told my driver sarcastically that these are the kinds of guys who'll survive when the apocalypse comes. Then we ourselves crashed into another vehicle and I got out to check on the passengers. There was a woman in the driver's seat. She looked at me vacantly while holding a baby with blue lips to her nipple. The baby looked dead. The woman looked down at the passenger seat. There was something wrapped in a blanket. One of the lads on the bridge shouted menacingly: Don't touch it! I unwrapped the blanket. It was a newborn boy, raw and red, who smiled at me in a familiar way and spoke to me like an adult. I had the impression he was saying something important but I couldn't understand him.

I have things to say, or think I do, but as I sit on the bench in the garden with my notebook or take my seat at the computer I split in two, watch myself start to write, formalise the act, and the moment of inspiration recedes until I'm left with—what? Writing about my failure to write, which feels like a moral failure.

Odd illusion, the sense of splitting in two, into actor and watcher, the one who lives and the ghostly double watching as if from beyond the grave. Odd, since there's no separation in nature—no isolated organisms, no ghosts looking on at the living. In nature, life and death are inseparable. Animals don't put the dying in hospices. They die where they lived, open to death.

Everywhere out here death intertwines with life, as any farmer knows. On the young beech trees along the path, last year's dead leaves mingle with this year's buds, which push them out and renew the cycle: on the same tree, both winter and summer, life and death. The trees across the field communicate and send nutrients to each other through underground webs of fungi that feed on dead plants and animals.

When a tree blossoms, death blossoms in it along with life, wrote Rilke. *And the animals patiently go from one to the other—and all around us death is at home.* It's only we who attempt the impossible movement of pushing death away from ourselves and so end up splitting ourselves in two. For Rilke, death is deep inside us, inescapable, and can't be tricked. But it only haunts us when we guard ourselves against it, only seems hostile when we turn from it. In the Open, there's no separation. The Open says yes to both life and death, affirms both presence and absence. It's here we have the chance to draw death back into us. Not in order to turn away from life and seek to die, but to live more truly, to be returned to the world as if in a second grace. We have the chance to draw the ghostly, hostile outside into what Rilke calls the *Weltinnenraum*, the world's inner space:

> Through all beings spreads *one* space:
> the world's inner space. The birds fly silently
> through us. Oh, I who want to grow,
> I look outside, and inside me the tree grows.
>
> I care, and the house stands inside me.
> I take shelter, and the shelter is inside me.

In the *Weltinnenraum* the outside is in and the inside out, but not as in Beckett's and Blanchot's dispersals, and not as in the daily distractions to which we willingly subject ourselves. Here, says Rilke,

it seems that everything
makes us at home. Look, the trees *are*; the houses
that we live in are still here.

This journal is no longer a hard slog. It's a little lighter, a little easier. Now if I can't get to it for a while, if I get a big job or no peace to think, I start to crave returning to the work that matters. When I do, it's a physical relief.

Leafing through another notebook the other day—rarely a good idea—I found this, written a decade ago:

Endless work. What's your real work? You ask the question so often the question itself becomes a form of work. You tunnel through a mountain of other people's words and smuggle out your own dubious hoard with no destination in sight. Always adrift between your beginning and end.

But today this, from W.S. Graham:

With words my material and immediate environment I am at once halfway the victim and halfway the successful traveller. There is the involuntary war between me and that environment flowing in on me from all sides and there is the poetic outcome. I am not the victim of my environment. History does not repeat itself. I am the bearer of that poetic outcome. History continually arrives as differently as our most recent minute on earth. The labourer going home in the dusk shouts his goodnight across the road and History has a new score on its track. The shape is changed a little.

The builders are making a racket, drilling into the ground where the old farm was, pouring cement from a huge revolving mixer, and laying a foundation. But the birds are still singing. S. looks at the birdsong transliterations in her fieldbook to try to identify them, and downloads an audio guide to make sure she's right. It's Greek to me, but it fills me with love to watch her patiently learning.

From the same old notebook:

I wake up tired of waking up. Lured into another endless day, the last day begun again. There's something I've missed, some fatal flaw in my reasoning that prevents me moving from here to the real vantage point, to real life. I see no path to take. What would it look like? Where would it go? It would end up back here, in dead time.

Nothing to say and the guilt of not filling time, which makes you speak to yourself in their words: "Stop inventing little hardships to make yourself look interesting. Get a proper job. Get a life. Get laid."

I could take up a hobby to at least look active, like sailing. Master wind and tide and all that. Grow a big beard. But I'd have to learn and I'm not the learning type. And imagine all the fuss, all the tarring and rigging and straining. Or maybe I should get a pet. That's what people do, isn't it? Something to care for, a loyal dog to walk. But then I'd have to get up early, hoover more, go to the vet, pick up poo. And I wouldn't be able to travel. Not that I do anyway.

So easy to drag yourself down like this. So hard to get back up!

As bleak as winter was, so lush is early summer. The contrast is stunning. We veer off the paths while we still can, before the vegetation grows too thick. The breeze is warm and the sunlight plays on leaves, blades of grass, the wings of insects. The air is thick with pollen. To layman's eyes like mine, it's a nice, tranquil scene at first sight. But I'm aware from my old naturalist friends that these woods are alive with millions of specific, urgent activities, only a tiny fraction of which I can see or understand. I do know that the bluebells and cowslips are blooming; that hoverflies, bees, and butterflies are out in abundance. A squirrel screeches. Jays mob something in a tree: maybe a sparrowhawk or kestrel, says S. She spots finches, warblers, early swifts, some rarer bird whose name escapes me now. She tells me they might be on their second or even third broods already. A muntjac stops and stares at us with wide eyes until a pair of playful squirrels scares it off. We walk back to the cottage full of sun and life.

Wallace Stevens: *After the final no there comes a yes / And on that yes the future world depends.*

S. has been going to weekly meditation sessions at a Zen Buddhist priory in Norwich for a month. She's started meditating in the living room every morning too, using an app that makes gong sounds. She sits on a pillow on the floor, looking at the wall. I make sure to stay quiet in the bedroom. Once a month the prioress gives a lecture about some aspect of Zen. This month's lecture, S.'s first, was about right effort, one part of the Eightfold Path. S. says it was to do with finding a middle way between applying too little and too much effort in meditation, between being distracted by your thoughts and trying to control them. The prioress said that when you apply right effort, you might experience what she called *openings*. What did she mean by that? I ask S. I'm not quite sure, says S., it was something about the loosening of the grip of the self and seeing the interconnectedness of things. But she also said that when you describe it abstractly you push it into a goal to be reached, when what you're looking for is already here.

End of the month. Jobs finished, invoices sent, dishes done. Now a free, sunny afternoon spreads out before me. Bliss! I take two translations of Kafka's Zurau aphorisms and the laptop out to the petal-strewn garden, and sit with bees buzzing around me and flies landing on the screen.

Kafka's aphorisms shed light on his fiction and reveal him as an original and troubling religious writer. He wrote most of them in his sister's house in the Bohemian countryside after he was first diagnosed with tuberculosis. He thought he was dying and wanted to become clear about *the last things*, to resolve questions that had grown urgent, away from the torments of the office and the noise of the city. He'd later see this as the happiest time of his life.

After the labourers' lunchbreak, the construction work starts again. I go back inside to get my earplugs, sit down, copy out and make notes on some of those glacial, enigmatic sayings that have been with me for so long, turning and returning in my head.

You're the task. No student far and wide. You're the problem to be solved, the experiment that must come into its own. No student in sight to work on you. No curriculum or method. If there's a teacher or taskmaster, he isn't mentioned. The material you're given to work with is what's closest to hand, so close it's hard to see clearly, and impossible to see from a neutral vantage point.

There are only two things: the truth and the lie. The truth is indivisible, so cannot know itself. Anyone who seeks to know it must be a lie. You can't know the truth because you're in the way of it. Moreover: *Only evil has self-knowledge.* You couldn't know yourself even if you were in the truth. This would seem to make the task that you are impossible.

There is nothing but a spiritual world; what we call the world of the senses is the evil in the spiritual, and what we call evil is only a requirement of a moment in our everlasting development. This is Kafka at his most Gnostic. The world and the body are transitory prisons which must be escaped if we're to attain eternal life, but from which escape seems impossible since we're enmeshed in them—in lies.

Only through self-destruction can the lie of the world be escaped: If, having gained knowledge, you want to attain eternal life—and you cannot do other than want to, for knowledge is this desire—then you must destroy yourself, the obstacle. This version of Kafka counsels absolute failure in the face of the world: *Fail to know yourself! Destroy yourself!*

In the struggle between you and the world, second the world. Kafka writes: *sekundiere der Welt.* One translator writes: *hold the world's coat.* Assist the world of the senses in its duel against you. Help it destroy you in order to spiritualise yourself.

But, as Ritchie Robertson suggests: *There is a counter-current in Kafka's thought: the idea that possibly the world of the senses can after all be made acceptable.* How? Knowledge is the desire for eternal life, for the triumph of the spiritual over the sensual. But again, anyone who seeks to know the truth must be a lie. How to resolve this conflict? Is there a way to seek the truth and be in the world at once?

One of Kafka's diary entries reads: *Contemplation and activity have their apparent truth; but only the activity radiated by contemplation, or rather, that which returns to it again, is truth.* Thinking and doing, looking on from the outside versus acting in the world: both have their place, their apparent truths, but only in their continual return to each other and their mutual illumination can truth happen, in an interweaving of the spiritual and the sensual. (And isn't writing a space in which contemplation and activity can come together as an event or even weapon of truth?)

In a handful of aphorisms, Kafka speaks of what he calls the indestructible: *Theoretically there is a perfect possibility of happiness: believing in the indestructible in oneself and not striving towards it.* Not pursuing it like a goal but trusting it without second-guessing, and going humbly about your life. In a letter, Kafka rewrites this sentence, replacing *the indestructible* with *the decisive divine.*

This *Unzerstörbare* is impersonal yet individual:

A person cannot live without a steady faith in something indestructible within him, though both the faith and the indestructible thing may remain permanently concealed from him. One of the forms of this concealment is the belief in a personal god.

The indestructible, and the possibility of free and true being, is in each person, concealed but real, something both individualising and uniting. It's not unlike the principle of *atman* in Hinduism, the spark of the divine hidden in each person.

The indestructible is one: it is each individual human being and, at the same time, it is common to all, hence the incomparably indivisible union that exists between human beings.

But what if, for whatever reason, this trust, this connection to the indestructible in oneself, has been severed, as it had for Kafka? (*The way to my neighbour is very long,* he writes elsewhere.) How to recover it? There's no technique for attaining true being in Kafka's idiosyncratic theology. Despite its affinity with Gnosticism, it's not a hermetic teaching or a path for the elect. There are no secret Kabbalistic rites through which the initiated can access the indestructible. Kafka never defines the word. Nor can it be commanded by reason, though sometimes *the right word, the right name* may invoke it. *This is the essence of magic,* he writes in his diary, *which does not create but summons.*

Kafka links the indestructible with *life's splendour*, with paradise:

> If what is supposed to have been destroyed in paradise was destructible, then it was not decisive; but if it was indestructible, then we are living in a false belief.

This false belief, in Roberto Calasso's words, has to do with a basic misunderstanding about why we were expelled from paradise: *Humans are convinced that they were kicked out of that place for eating the fruit of the Tree of Knowledge of Good and Evil. But this is an illusion. That wasn't their sin. Their sin lay in not yet having eaten from the Tree of Life.*

Our trial is continual. It's the conflict between our limited, deceptive knowledge and the veiled essence of being within us. But if being is indestructible, says Kafka, then it's possible that our expulsion stems from our own illusions and that in fact we're still in paradise *whether we know it or not.* And that the way to return to where and who we are, to bridge thought and being, to find the way back to our neighbour, goes through the *mad strength of faith*, which he does define:

> Faith means: freeing the indestructible in yourself or better: freeing yourself or better: being indestructible or better: being.

Part of the reason why Kafka struggled against the world of the senses—of family, sex, marriage, and community—is that he saw writing as his supreme spiritual vocation, for which all else had to be sacrificed. In a letter to the father of his fiancée Felice, explaining why he couldn't marry her, he wrote:

My whole being is directed towards literature; I have followed this direction unswervingly until my thirtieth year, and the moment I abandon it I cease to live. Everything I am, and am not, is a result of this. I am taciturn, unsociable, morose, selfish, a hypochondriac, and actually in poor health. Fundamentally I deplore none of this: it is the earthly reflection of a higher necessity.

Like Kafka, Rilke often felt caught between writing and life, but moved more naturally towards unifying them. He saw his writing as springing from daily life, inseparable from it. In a letter, he wrote:

In the end, everyone experiences only one conflict in life, which constantly reappears in different forms. Mine is to reconcile life with work in the purest sense; and when it comes to the infinitely incommensurable work of the artist, there the two directions are opposed... But for me not even asceticism is possible. Since my productivity stems from the simplest veneration of life, from a daily, endless amazement before it... I would see it as a lie to refuse any of the currents flowing towards me; for no matter how much art might gain from it, every such refusal must eventually be expressed as hardness and take revenge within the art itself: for who can be open and accepting on such delicate ground if they have a distrustful, hemmed-in, and fearful attitude towards life!

Wild, screaming swifts over Kirkwood. The most birdlike of birds, I always think when I see them in flight. They spend almost their entire lives in the air. We like to watch them feed at dusk, before they soar up to a height the raptors can't reach and sleep on the wing.

I've found the patch in the woods where the muntjacs live; I guess they don't move around much. I can usually find them if I'm careful, but I try to stem my desire to stalk them, so they won't flee. I love to know they're there, living their secret lives, and I think of them often. Their eyes when they see you are different from the pleading eyes of a dog in a pub: they want nothing from you, only to be left alone.

Rookie comes home with scratches and missing fur. Another cat has turned up on his patch. We've seen the two of them crouched at opposite ends of the garden, yowling and eyeing one another with ominously swaying tails. S. tries to clean Rookie's wounds, but he wriggles out of her hands and hisses at her.

The trees are letting their seeds fly in the wind. White catkin fluff catches to things like sheep's wool on brambles. I picked some from my beard this morning. The scatter-approach to pollination: something's bound to take in the earth and grow lasting and solid, as if it was always there.

When I can't write, when the building noise distracts me or when I have nothing to say, I so easily get outside myself. I'm not at home. Writing is a house of being under construction; sometimes you feel you're living in rubble. But then the right sentence comes, the edifice rises up around you, and it is what was there all along. When this happens, the world lies open. You can get up from your desk and live in your home, kiss S., make plans with her.

Writing isn't just a hall of mirrors, as I once thought. Nor is it a game. A sentence, even a banal one, when brought out of contemplation and written down, can be a practical act in its own way, like an act of faith. What happens when you write down a thought, when you start to blacken the screen? Often your subject eludes you. The words disperse. But doesn't something happen nevertheless? No matter how unsure you are of what you're saying, no matter how badly you fail to grasp it, doesn't something take place in the saying itself that can give you strength to go on?

When we go through the woods, says Heidegger, we're always already going through the word *woods*. Both the woods and the word were there before us, but it's the going through them that brings them together. In a sense, the saying of the word summons the thing. Summons but doesn't create. We can't give being, but we can help unveil it.

But what is it that sometimes appears when word and thing come together? What glints on the other side of being? Celan once wrote that he saw God in a ray of light under his hotel door. Is it something like that: a ray of light under the door of a dark rented room?

On windless evenings at sunset, when the birds stop singing and nothing moves or rustles, before the nocturnal animals come out of their hiding places and the heavy silence of night falls, the landscape seems to sink into a concentrated stillness, as if it's listening for something.

Boundless blue sky. Quiet happiness again, like an advent. Some days there seem to be hints of a hidden God everywhere. When I do the dishes or walk to the shops, even when I chat with S. A God of intimations, a last God which may or may not come, when all other gods have passed away. It's hard to write about. We can talk about being with some boldness, even stake some claim in it, but how dare to talk about God?

Beyond the word God, even beyond being, God withdraws—into God. Eckhart wrote: *Whatever one says that God is, he is not; he is what one does not say of him, rather than what one says he is.* And: *God is a being beyond being and a nothingness beyond being. God is nothing. No thing. God is nothingness. And yet God is something.*

We can say nothing worthy of God—if we deign to believe—but we can try however clumsily with the words that come, and some truth may be given to us in our approach. Something may pass fleetingly through time. I remember that summer afternoon in the cool musty church. The impersonal light through the stained-glass window. I felt an overfacing power and I felt it withdraw. What they used to call faith, blooming out of nothing.

The hot sun draws out all the life hidden in the earth under a huge, cloudless sky: every weed and blade of grass, every flower, every insect. The closer you look at this quiet fold of country, the richer in life it is, and the richer in death. The other day S. said that even a biologist probably wouldn't be able to catalogue in a lifetime all that's happening in a small patch of these woods.

Heatwave. It's all anyone can talk about. It's as if a glass dome has been lowered over Broadland. There's no escape. It hasn't rained for a month and Norfolk is already one of the driest counties in the country. People seem weighed down. Water levels have dropped, leaving ugly stains on banks and sluices. The fields and meadows are yellow and crunchy underfoot, and birds, mammals, and insects are flocking to the rivers. The blackberries are ripe a month early.

We've bought a fan and lie sweltering on the bed and sofa with our hot computers on our laps. If this is what it's like here, I say to S., imagine what it's like in Delhi, or Riyadh. What's it going to be like in fifty years? A hundred? Norfolk might be underwater by then, she says.

The effects of the feedback loop we've created are now playing out in real time: the papers report droughts, floods, and wildfires all over the world. Polar ice is melting and reflecting less heat from the sun, ocean surfaces are expanding and absorbing more. As the seas warm and rise, earthquakes and hurricanes are becoming commonplace. Freshwater around the planet is drying up. Crops are baking in the sun. Overheated forests are starting to release rather than absorb carbon dioxide, raising temperatures further. Species are dying out thousands of times faster than their natural extinction rate. We can still ignore things for now, still enjoy ourselves, worry about our careers and relationships, raise children. But unless we arrest the loop, extreme weather will dwarf our lives and the resources we need for our own survival will be lost for good.

It's nature taking its revenge on us, we say. And so we continue our crafty habit of imposing our own stories on it, as if it were a force separate from us which, if angered, will strike us down. As if the world were a battlefield.

I wake up feeling cramped. The mood stays with me all day while I work to meet a tight deadline. The project manager rushes me. When I've hit SEND I'm at a loss. What's been accomplished here? The work is anonymous and I don't know where it's going or who's going to read it, if anyone. Too tired for my real work. And now the day's passing like so many others, like smoke in the wind. I need a drink.

Walking to the Rose, I think of those lines by Burroughs that sometimes come back to me when I feel this way, from the book with the corny slang: *Kick is seeing things from a special angle. Kick is momentary freedom from the claims of the aging, cautious, nagging, frightened flesh.* Seductive words. He was talking about drugs, about escaping the prison of the body, until you drop back down and immediately crave some more. As seductive as a preacher, I think, as I try to catch the bartender's eye. Gnostic salvation from the flesh. *Soma-sema*, body as tomb. The battle between mind and body.

Enough of that. Finish your pint. Go home and say something nice to S., feed Rookie, make a good dinner. Don't let the day pass without a trace.

In the caff with N., I overhear some visiting birders talking about nightjars. Apparently they're breeding on Buxton Heath and you can see them at dusk. N. offers to drive me and S. there in his van. I ring S. to ask if she wants to come. She says yes, but she has to send a couple of emails first. We linger over our pot of tea, then pick her up.

Wandering down the heath, we see some people with binoculars who whisper to us that they've spotted them. We hear the distinctive, earthy croaking from branches where the birds sit in their perfect tree-bark disguises. Some of them will already have settled on their ground nests, S. tells me. We stand still and silent for a few minutes in the blue light. I get bored and start to roll a cigarette but one of the birders waves his finger and whispers that it's too dry. Then he points at the sky and we catch a couple of nightjars displaying in surprisingly elegant flight, the male flashing the white stripes on his long wings. I didn't know they could fly so well, I say to S. when they're out of sight. Well they've flown from Africa, she says. I had no idea. The man who spotted them is animated. In all my years of birding I've never seen a display like that, he whispers. We wait around for a while, then head back up the sandy path to the carpark. In a dreamlike moment, a herd of black horses trots past us. Some of them stop and nudge us with their muzzles. We stand still with our hands behind our backs until they move on.

As we drive back, a hood of clouds moves over us, but it's still hot outside. We stop at the Rose. When we've sat down with our drinks there's a sudden chill and a long roll of thunder. Rain! It falls heavily. The pressure lifts from the air. People come alive and start chatting and laughing. We go outside, stand with our arms outstretched, and get drenched.

Bachelard described what he called the poetic instant as *a simultaneity in which the most scattered and disunited being achieves unity.* He saw it as an ambivalent moment, both surprising and familiar, which breaks up everyday time and gathers in its contradictory events: a vertical time in which *being rises or descends without accepting world time.* In the poetic instant, he says, *flat horizontality suddenly vanishes. Time no longer flows. It spouts.* He also used the image of a sailboat held in balance by the opposing forces of the waves against its hull and the wind in its sail. When this happens, the hull is said to hum.

Similarly, Merleau-Ponty described time—phallically—as a fountain that surges upward in a kind of eternal present rather than flowing horizontally like a river. He spoke of time as ceaselessly welling up within us whether we like it or not. But even though we can't escape its upsurging, it doesn't leave us powerless, since one can *find a remedy against it in itself, as happens in a decision which binds me or in the act of establishing a concept.* We can choose to root our consciousness in time by *taking up a situation* in the present, thereby renewing our *primitive alliance* with the world. *Time exists for me because I have a present,* Merleau-Ponty says, *and the present (in the wide sense, along with its horizons of primary past and future)... enjoys a privilege because it is the zone in which being and consciousness coincide.*

The moment that opens up the world to you, once you've found words to name it. Wouldn't it be a kind of torment otherwise, the slow arc of your life? But you know what that's like. Empty time. As if you'd lived the same life many times over and drained it of meaning. A ghostly life, as in Kafka's story about Gracchus, the long-dead hunter whose barge was meant to take him to the beyond before it was blown off course, and who now floats aimlessly at sea, unable to live or die. Time flattened out. The sense that no matter what you do, you'll be just as bored as before. Your boredom reaches such a pitch that now it's only a small step—to what? You can almost see it: a time that knows nothing of boredom. You can almost see it: a kind of grace.

Rilke: *When things become difficult and unbearable, we find ourselves in a place already very close to its transformation.*

What was the planetary time, the time of the day I tried to understand when I first came out here, when I started this journal? Didn't I see it in the empty fields, the drifts of clouds, the way Rookie sat on the windowsill for hours with his eyes closed? The same seasons over and over, the years stretching into sameness. The dreaded tedium of the day, relieved by distractions I was only too happy to sign up to.

As if time could be put at a distance so easily. The seasons aren't the same as your everyday routines, the day isn't your day, however similar they sometimes seem. They tell you: find your own time.

There appears to be no universal flow of time in nature shared by every species. Planetary time—what is that to creatures who live in bodies? Different species perceive time in different ways depending on how their perceptual apparatuses have developed. The fly in my study reacts up to four times faster than I do when I try to swat it. Some of the birds outside my window sing and interpret each other's calls at speeds our hearing can't follow. Perhaps their lives seem as long to them as ours do to us, since they live them so much faster. In any event they live in different times, at home in the times of their species in ways that make us look maladapted. We don't share a time with our own species, and less and less even with ourselves. But we have the potential, perhaps, to experience time more deeply than any other species we share the planet with, and thereby rediscover our links to them.

I sense the moment of being waiting, somewhere near, to return me to myself, hold me in my course and sustain the slow arc of my life; waiting to show me that time isn't just some vast universal drift out there in the world, isn't just the seasonal time of my species, but is what I'm made of.

I call the moment a return, but isn't it more like a repetition? A daily repetition, like a prayer, that makes the same new and lets you face the future, lets you function in the world.

Kierkegaard wrote about repetition, about redoubling and transforming your past as a way of choosing your own life. But for Kierkegaard, repetition, *gentagelse*, means more than wresting the past into the present and changing it by force of will. True repetition points both backward and forward in time: it renews your past while opening it up to the unknown, and ultimately to the eternal. It's a kind of suspension of time that lets you accept your past and gives it back to you as something new, as when Job in the Old Testament was given back his former life and more when everything seemed impossible to bear. It's an act of faith in life that's experienced as a gift, not taken.

My mother calls to talk about my father. Since he retired he's been having trouble walking, and is now bedridden, taking strong painkillers, and losing weight. After countless tests, the doctors have finally concluded that the nerves in his legs are irreparably damaged by blood clots. My mother asks us to visit. I catch S.'s attention, cup the phone with my hand, and ask her if she wants to go to Denmark. She thinks for a second, then says yes. After I hang up, we buy flights and train tickets for the following week. I've been feeling a nostalgic urge to see my old places in Denmark anyway. It occurs to me now that this feeling must have something to do with all this talk of returning and repetition.

The week passes with work, housework, gardening, cooking, making love, watching films, lazing about with Rookie. We clean the pantry and bring in the fruit and veg sign from the road. I'm comfortable, too comfortable maybe, but it's a good change. I sense the power of the moment and the eternal God in the backdrop of everyday life.

At the airport in Copenhagen, it always strikes me how much cleaner and well-built everything is than in Britain. We take the metro to my parents' flat. After we've showered, I unpack while S. helps my mother make dinner. My father eats with shaking hands. Things are difficult for him now. He's lost some of his power, his familiarity with the world. He almost seems like an ordinary man.

In the morning we fix their bikes, which they haven't used for years. S. cycles to the library to work while I cycle to the central station and take the coastal train up to my old hometown. I want to retrace the little groove of the life I left there.

Everything's more or less the same, except that the vegetation has grown and as a result the place seems to have matured, come into its own. When I lived here as a child it was a new, rather sterile suburb, planned and built in the sixties like so many others to accommodate the booming post-war generation, replacing the old fishing community. Later, when I returned to live here again with my family after my father's posting in Canada came to an end (and after I'd spent a year at a boarding school), I spent so much empty time waiting to grow up, in the house and wandering the paths, the coastline, and the forest, imagining my future self looking back on me with mixed feelings.

I suspected by coming back I might be indulging a flimsy fantasy, but now I feel the past gather up in me. It's the same, this place, and so am I, in some essential way the same as I was then. I go into the library where I used to sit and read, to the supermarket where I worked; I don't know anyone in there now, of course. Then I cycle down the old paths. The hills seem smaller, as I thought they might. Our old house has been done up with a new roof and garage. There's no one around. Everything is still, the houses seem almost abandoned. Now I remember what it was like: a typical Danish suburb. It used to give me what Burroughs, when he was stuck in villages during his travels in South America, called the fear of stasis, of being *just where I am and nowhere else,* under *the dead weight of time.* But today, somehow, it's deeply satisfying. I cycle through the old beech forest where I played with my childhood friends, and down to the harbour where I order a crab sandwich from the old fishmongers and eat it on the pier while looking out at the Sound and the Swedish shore.

The next day we go to Lejre, near Roskilde, where there's a Viking museum that S. found online. I've never been and know nothing about it. We take the bikes on the train and cycle through the countryside to the museum, stopping to scrump from apple trees by the road. It's the landscape around the museum that impresses us most, with its glacier-formed hills and valleys, prehistoric passage graves, the remains of Viking longhouses, and burial sites marked out with huge stones arranged in the form of ships designed to carry the dead to *hel*. The rolling country doesn't look very Danish to me, but it turns out to be the mythical and historical centre of Denmark: it's the seat of the legendary Skjöldung dynasty, in whose great hall *Beowulf* begins, as well as the seat of real medieval kings and bishops who presided over busy settlements. I ask S., the historian, why they settled here rather than by the fjord. I don't know, she says, maybe it was more fertile, or they knew about the prehistoric graves, realised it was a sacred site and took it over.

I've never felt the presence of ancient history as strongly, even when seeing bog bodies in museums. There's something about these remains and monuments being left alone on open land that's surprisingly moving. People lived here with their animals, worked in the fields, argued, laughed, raised children. I wonder if any of their descendants settled in Norfolk. In the museum itself, the star exhibit is a tiny silver statuette of Odin seated on a throne flanked by raven messengers, found in this ground like all the other objects on display.

As we set off on our bikes to go back to the station we pass an unusual number of rooks, jackdaws, and hooded crows in the fields. It's still sunny; they can't be starting to roost. It occurs to me they may well be the descendants of birds that scavenged Iron Age and Viking fields and middens, *møddinger*. Is it possible that they have some ancient attachment to the place?

While S. works, my mother drives me to my grandparents' old farm to see how the restoration is coming along. It's taken forever, she says. I remember that someone acquired it after my grandparents died, and ran a workshop in the barn, but left the house as it was, crumbling away. It was always sad to drive by. Since then, my mother says, someone else bought it and now it's being made into a villa. I'm curious to see it, and to see if the countryside looks the same.

It does. And the farm has been superbly restored. The walls are as white as they must have been originally, and the layout has been kept as it was. It's no longer a farm, of course, but they still keep chickens in the same yard. We drive down the old dirt lane to get a closer look. My mother seems pleased. I wonder what's in the barn now, I say. She gets a vacant look.

We drive further down, towards the neighbouring farm. An old man in dungarees with a cigarette behind his ear is fiddling with something in a shed by the lane. He stands up stiffly and says, Can I help you? My mother calls him by his name and he looks at her suspiciously. When she tells him who she is, his eyes light up. We get out of the car and they chat about the old times while I light a cigarette. Is this your son? he asks. It is, I say, and I remember you too; I used to run around here with my air rifle. Is that really you? he says. He tells us his farm was sold many years ago and that he lives in a flat now, but he likes to come and help when he feels up to it. He takes us down to the farm, where we buy strawberries and potatoes from the new owners.

On the way back to Copenhagen, I ask my mother about her childhood. She tells me stories I've heard and some I haven't. Her parents grew up on big family-owned farms in Jutland that went bankrupt during the Depression. After they married, they travelled to Zealand, where her father found a job running a farm as a leaseholder. They had two children: my aunt and my mother. My mother remembers her father tilling his fields with a horse-drawn plough and, when he got a tractor, standing on the back of the seed-spreader and helping him sow. My mother and aunt took the route of many young women from the country: they went to Copenhagen and got jobs as secretaries. My mother met my father, and my aunt met a British businessman who took her with him back to London, where they married and had a son, who now runs a media agency in the City. It's hard to believe that only two generations ago our grandfather was ploughing with a horse.

It's common to dismiss nostalgia as a longing for a past that never was. We're taught—indoctrinated—to look forward, be proactive and innovative, shape our own futures, never stand still. But doesn't nostalgia have its place as a way of recovering one's past? A past that may not have been fully lived can gain deeper meaning when it's revisited, and enrich the present. And can't looking forward become an empty gesture if your past and present aren't gathered up in it?

Heidegger writes somewhere that *origin always comes to meet us from the future*. Strange saying. What does it mean? Perhaps that time, rather than moving in a straight line from past to future, or from here to the afterlife, describes a kind of circle between the future and the past that can bring us back to the moment of presence if we attend to it closely enough.

I make plans, anticipate my future, and what comes back to me from the future is my entire past, demanding that I accept it as my own.

Back in Kirkwood we wake to a clear warm morning. In the afternoon it rains and in the evening you can see your breath. It's as if the day is showing us every season. For the first time I can take pleasure in autumn, in the slow waning of the year.

The Greeks called the straight line of time from past to future *chronos*. But, for them, time was twofold: its other element was *kairos*, the decisive moment. *Chronos* was world time that carries on regardless of us, *kairos* the personal experience of time. In classical rhetoric, *kairos* meant finding the right words at the right time.

For Paul, *kairos* had to do with the fullness of time realised in the Incarnation, the moment of conversion, and the imminent arrival of the Kingdom of Heaven. It was the intersection of history and eternity, the time when God acted in the world and inaugurated a new age. The task of the Christian was, in imitation of Christ, to keep the eternal God always in his heart on his passage through earthly life, to be *wakeful* and *pray without ceasing*, and in this way help fulfil God's will on Earth in the here and now.

Only with the moment does history begin, wrote Kierkegaard. He described the moment—*øjeblikket*, the glance of the eye, or the moment of seeing—as *an atom of eternity*:

> The moment is that ambiguity in which time and eternity touch each other, and with this the concept of temporality is posited, whereby time constantly intersects eternity and eternity constantly pervades time.

A moment as such is unique. To be sure, it is short and temporal, as the moment is; it is passing, as the moment is, past, as the moment is in the next moment, and yet it is decisive, and yet it is filled with the eternal. A moment such as this must have a special name. Let us call it: the fullness of time.

Now on my walks I stop by our local church. I like the routine. I like the heavy wooden door, the cold stone slabs on the floor, even the musty air. There are children's drawings on the peeling walls, dull parish notices, faded black-and-white photos. I sit on a pew for a few minutes, leaf through a hymn book or a Bible, look at the altar, the wooden rafters like the ribs of an old ship, the stained-glass window showing Christ with two fingers raised to symbolise the hypostatic union. (How many people argued, lived, and died for that idea!) Relics, I sometimes think. Yet still here in the ruins, on the same ground as the rest of us.

Eternal God, which makes the moment seem like a grain of sand... Where's the divine *kairos* now, when God no longer acts in the world, when the God of men has died? Where's the intersection of time and eternity? When is the right time, what's the right word? I can't call it *him*, I can't call it *you*. But doesn't the moment hint at it? Doesn't it whisper to us of it? Often I think the moment whispers something too terrible to hear, something I secretly want no part of, that might overturn my whole life.

Yet you've felt it, haven't you? A power that made everything you are both meaningless and meaningful. Room to breathe, a sense of dignity. As long as you were shielded by time, held in the perfect stillness of the moment. How carefully it has to be approached. But maybe that's not the right word. Questioned, perhaps. Or undergone.

I sometimes think, to comfort myself, that God withdrew from the world at the moment of creation, leaving space to let the world come into its own, in its own time, and seek its source the way plants turn to face the sun.

The construction work on T.'s old farm is coming along. Having demolished the house, haybarn, and cowshed, and removed the rubble, they're building something that looks like a barn conversion, as well as a double garage, and they've also started landscaping. I look up the planning permission and find the developer's website, which says: *Many people aspire to live in barn conversions. But the opportunities to convert or renovate an existing barn are limited—there are only so many of them. And it can be expensive. That's why a barn-style house is becoming an increasingly popular option.*

The double who stood beside me as I typed... When did he turn up? There was a carpark and a concrete path between thistle bushes. I shook my father's hand, turned away, started walking back to my room in the boarding school. A room in a corridor full of strangers speaking a language that no longer came naturally to me. In that moment, on the path, I felt as if split in two. I was a walking body and an abstract observer. I've since heard of other, much worse experiences, during which people felt as if they were leaving their bodies and looking down at what was happening to them. People who spent the rest of their lives trying to reverse that moment.

I was maladjusted: that's what my mother told me years later when I asked her why they sent me away to a Danish boarding school in the middle of nowhere. I'd taken up with the wrong crowd in Canada, was on my way to becoming a criminal. That was true in a sense. So boarding school was what I needed, I supposed, or what I deserved. When I wasn't in class I hid in my room and drank beer, went to the library in town and took out CDs, or rode my bike to the forest. I barely spoke. I spoke halting Danish now anyway, still thought in English. I became sensitive to the slightest noise: footsteps in the corridor, voices in the bathroom, a knock on a door. Mostly the corridor was eerily silent. Then there'd be a flurry of activity that made me start; then silence again. I didn't answer knocks on my door. I'd overhear people talking about me, about the guy who never left his room and listened to weird music. On the weekends I'd escape to my grandparents' old farm in the country, where I watched TV or cycled to the coast on my grandfather's ancient bike. I'd sit on the pier looking at the sea. Sometimes I'd read or listen to my discman, but mostly I just sat there, without the words to explain what was happening to me.

It's freezing. On a walk we find the feathers of a pheasant savaged by a fox or bird of prey. S. collects the tail feathers and some branches. When we get home, she arranges them in a vase.

What happened after the double turned up? One of Blanchot's narrators talks of being *represented in my feelings by a double for whom each feeling was as absurd as for a dead person.* On the path between the thistle bushes there was me, another me, and a haze that began to gather between me and the world, that stayed with me for a long time, and gave things a distant, dreamlike quality. When I spoke to people, my words seemed to come from far away, while the double, I imagined, stood by with a smirk.

What seems clear to me now is that something goes wrong for everyone. One way or another, suddenly or slowly, of our own will or by force, we go astray. We lose sight of some essential part of ourselves; hide from being. But we can never close ourselves off from it completely, never lose our link to the unity we spring from. How could we? Michel Haar writes: *We are held in being, and no matter how tenuous the thread attaching us to presence—for example in fainting or dreamless sleep—we are never, as long as we are, released into pure nothingness.* Never released from the link to being that lets us become our more or less divided selves and live on the same ground as all other beings, no matter how different from us.

We arrange to go north, to the Lancashire uplands, to spend Christmas with S.'s family. I get a key to the cottage cut for N. and ask him to come and feed Rookie. The next morning we call a taxi before sunrise, then take three trains. The passengers get chattier as the landscape becomes hillier. People are friendlier up north, says S.

I manage to sleep a little. It's dark and rainy when we arrive at the final station, where S.'s father is waiting for us in the car to drive us to S.'s family home. I look out the window while we chat. It seems as though every available space has been paved over and built up, apart from the great dark moors that loom above the villages, many of which are themselves man-made, the results of deforestation by ancient peoples. Nothing but motorways, roundabouts, malls, petrol stations, business parks, offices, terraced houses—all so grey and hard and closed in. I can't help but think of those lines by Hopkins again. Is there anywhere that isn't seared with trade, smeared with toil, dominated by capital? Is there any escape?

But S.'s family is large and fun. We eat, drink, and laugh all night. Her brother rolls a joint and passes it around. I get a disagreeable sensation of floating above myself and looking down at the gathering as if it were a scene in a film, which reminds me why I stopped smoking cannabis many years ago.

When we go to bed, I reveal my thoughts about the journey to S. It's the home of the industrial revolution after all, she says. Don't judge it just yet. You'll see.

The next morning is brighter and gives us a fine view of the hills on both sides of the road: swells of earth scattered with spray-painted sheep and crowned in mist. I go outside to smoke, feeling pleasantly small. There's a different quality to the silence here when there's no traffic. Something to do with the topography, maybe. I hear the trickling of a stream. A horse whinnies somewhere and it's as if being itself were briefly given voice.

This area has a Norse name, too: Rossendale, or "horse valley."

S. borrows her parents' car and drives us to Pendle Hill. We walk along the ridge through ribbons of fog to an ancient burial site she wants to see. Not a soul about, at last. As we climb the rocky path, dodging sheep droppings and sodden moss, we stop chatting and fall into a rhythm. Our minds relax and expand as the view widens. We stop to look out over rangy fields, reservoirs, and farmhouses. This is more like it, I tell S., you need a horizon to think. I love the dun colours, the reddish, iron-rich streams, the fat sheep that bound away heavily when we get too close— the total indifference of the place. It moves us both, and it's worth a day of rumbling through damp suburbs in crowded, dirty carriages.

Back in our workaday world in Kirkwood, Rookie sniffs our bags, spits at us, and ignores us for two days. At least he keeps the mice out, I tell S. The grudge is forgotten when I give him some smoked trout from the farm shop. After he's licked himself clean, he settles in his favourite place on the windowsill above the radiator. His neck is getting thick, his back muscular. I have to be careful when I give in to temptation and try to pet him.

On New Year's Eve, S. goes to a house party in Norwich while I clean the bathroom, shave, make soup from last night's chicken carcass, and read. Fireworks from the pub spray blue, green, and red flares across the black sky. I imagine the muntjacs and rabbits starting and running for cover, the sleeping birds fluttering off their perches.

In the morning, casual flakes of snow melt on the flagstones around a burnt-out rocket. S. returns, hungover, showers, and sits reading on the couch, wrapped in a blanket. We leave the heating on all day. Rookie knows which side of his bread is buttered: he's staying put on the windowsill till spring.

Winter is a season of routines. The days pass in almost the same way, especially out here. All we do is work, eat, walk, exercise, go to the pub, sleep. But this winter neither of us has been desperate for a holiday. I feel more and more, and S. does too, in her own way, that it doesn't matter whether you do the same things or new things, stay put or move about non-stop. Life is near and fresh. There are no ruts in nature, even in the barest places.

The gale blows me sideways along with the birds, branches, and grasses. The sleet makes no distinctions either: it whips into us all. Odd decision to take a walk in this weather, yet I feel as much a part of the landscape as ever. No longer separate but walking on the same open ground.

Early morning. The mist lifts and the trees, bushes, buildings, people come into focus. Learn to write—to think—like that, like the morning gathering itself out of a haze.

Last night I dreamt we'd sown a small plant that grew to waist-height overnight. We watched as its big oval leaves trembled and reached for the light. Look, I said to S., you can almost see it growing!

We go to Sheringham with N. and K. to see the Viking festival. Among the crowds are people dressed as Vikings. There's a procession during which some of them shout the names of Viking gods, and there's a mock Viking village where others demonstrate ancient Nordic crafts. N. is interested in the primitive iron forge at which a man is hammering an ornament into shape, stopping now and then to work the lever of the bellows. On the beach, in front of a replica longboat, two bands of warriors face off to re-enact a battle. Swords clang heavily against big wooden shields. A Viking on a loudspeaker explains that the name Sheringham derives from Norse and means *the ham of Scira's people*. Scira, he says, was a warlord who was given the village as a reward for his bravery in battle. The warriors run at each other and retreat until one of the bands is defeated. Striding up towards the town, past his slain enemies lying on wet sand, Scira lifts his sword in triumph and shouts at the crowd. We applaud and disperse.

The next day, on a walk, we pass a group of bored teenagers dressed in the nineties style that kids are into at the moment: puffy coats, baggy jumpers, white socks, and copies of trainers I recognise from my youth. A couple of boys even have floppy hair parted in the middle. One of them looks just like a friend of mine from when I was a teenager. There's a woman with them, talking about wildlife management: must be a biology daytrip. It's odd to see young people imitating the way we once dressed, while taking videos with their mobiles and wearing Bluetooth earphones.

It's not a great style to copy, is it, really? I say to S. when we're back home. But we Gen Xers didn't have much to work with. The idealism of the sixties, the rock-star decadence of the seventies, and the pop-star tackiness of the eighties were already being recycled in various ways, but many of us didn't believe in any of it. It didn't feel true to us. We were starting to see through the workings of the society the baby boomers had made. How could we not? We were a small generation pitched against masses of self-centred people busy shoring up their social capital at the expense of the rest of the world. Lots of us instinctively felt we were fucked, so we withdrew and became self-centred in our own ways while the boomers passed us over or absorbed us. We became bored and angry. For the committed slackers, even the label Generation X was lame, commercial. Yet it was fitting for a crossed-out generation. It meant: ignore us, we don't care, at least until we're absolutely forced to conform. We were hard to market to. What do you sell to people like that except Nirvana CDs?

And yet I watched former classmates become bankers, marketers, tech developers. I watched them compete for jobs, disappear into the vast corporate world, and devote their time to helping the boomers continue what they'd started. As did I, in my own small way. Is it any wonder so many of our successors, the millennials and Gen Z, seem so flighty, so prone to fads, self-branding, and burnout?

The boredom of those years—before diversions were available with the tap of a finger—never really left me. It mingled with the anxieties provoked by school, the need to impress and succeed, but it never really left. It grew, with the haze, into a feeling of general pointlessness. Even during fits of worry about exams, girls, or a wasted day, there was the sense of something neutral, something indifferent, that hovered over things and levelled all the events of life. I looked for ways to give this feeling substance, to turn it into something to live by. I read novels, went to plays, galleries, museums. I visited churches, temples, mosques. I went to London to study religion, but the feeling stayed with me and I dropped out after a year. Then I went to Norwich to study art and literature, thinking I might find what I needed there instead. I discovered more and more works of art, and people with similar interests to mine. And when we were taught to view the works we studied with suspicion, to take them apart and unpack their constitutive elements, it made sense to me. Wasn't that how I'd always felt, underneath it all? So-called meaning happened along arbitrary horizontal lines; one element along the line, however important the artist or author thought it was, could in principle be replaced with any of the others; it was almost impossible to *mean* something.

Meanwhile life still felt like a kind of photographic negative. But of what? What could the positive possibly mean now?

After doing a master's in translation, I found a flat in Norwich, worked in a chicken factory, and applied to translation agencies while my friends looked for academic jobs. When I started to get translation work I quit the factory, kept sending unsolicited applications, and made a meagre living translating difficult texts that other, more established translators declined.

My university friends moved away one by one. My life stalled. I went to Denmark once a year, but otherwise all I did was work and go to pubs. The days repeated themselves, blurred into sameness, interspersed by moments of desperation. How did people do it? I'd wonder. How did they get up in the mornings, do their tedious jobs and sit, sober, through the long evenings without topping themselves? What was surprising wasn't that some people took drugs, wandered the streets muttering, leapt off the roofs of buildings; it was that most people didn't.

I stayed in my flat, worked, drank, and slept. I stopped exercising, didn't write or read much; it was as if words had been emptied out, had lost their capacity to say anything of importance. Those years are fuzzy in my memory. In any case, not much happened. I've tried it all and failed, I thought, I failed or it failed, it doesn't matter, it's all the same. Whatever happened, it or I would fail, and so much the better. Better to dwell in failure than be duped by hope. In fact, I thought, I had a right, even a kind of duty, to accept failure in the face of all the fake positivity I saw around me, and in the texts I spent my days translating.

Something neutral and indifferent, which made every emotion seem absurd, every effort a non-starter... How to speak of it when *it* isn't a thing but more of a lack, a withdrawal of sense from the things we invest our feelings in?

In his book *Living with Indifference*, Charles E. Scott asks: *What is at stake for us as we live with a strong sense of indifference in the events of our lives?* What's at stake, perhaps, is our sanity. My projections fall short, my passions don't move the world. I can't get what I want. Something's kept hidden from me, the gate is shut and the gatekeeper isn't budging. I pretend I don't care, but it doesn't last. I'm no match for the world's indifference to me, and start to resent it. Scott describes what he calls patterns of denial that can develop when indifference is experienced as a threat, such as *an insistence on personalized and intentional universals... systematic tightness, emphasis on definitive closure... and a dominance of values of conformity.* Another path that's always open to me is to give up seeking a purpose in life, give into despair and try to find rest in failure, the conviction that no matter what I do it'll collapse. Or I can try to attend to indifference in a different way, leave myself open to it without losing faith in life, and see if something doesn't happen after all, in spite of everything. Scott describes ways of being *that can arise when people are aware of dimensions of indifference throughout their lives, and, far from being traumatized or obsessed by them, accept them and themselves with them, and develop, perhaps, values that take constructive account of those dimensions and the departures and beginnings that they occasion.*

It was when I'd climbed out of the hole, started my long walks and slimmed down, that I met S. She was a student at the time, and a friend of N.'s, whom she'd met in a stonemasonry course. When she graduated, she moved from her shared student house into my little one-bedroom flat. It soon got too small for the two of us and so we started to think about going elsewhere. We were both bothered by the noise from the road and the pub on the corner: the cars, the scrapes of kegs on the pavement, the sudden shouts from people sitting on the benches outside, the drunken midnight conversations under our windows. I needed peace and quiet like I needed food.

We hadn't thought about moving to the country, but when N. came to visit after he'd gone out to Kirkwood, he described the place to us and it started to seem like a good idea. We stayed with him for a weekend and went on walks together. When he called me one day and said there was a cottage to let near his place, I rang the agency straight away and arranged a viewing. Two days later we took the bus to Kirkwood and the minute we stepped in the door it felt right; it was as if the decision was made for us. It took a while to get used to living in Kirkwood, but we came to be grateful for the solitude and slowness of life here: the deep darkness at night, the brightness of the stars, the wild dawn chorus, the scents of the plants and flowers and soil.

The barn-style house is finished and the estate agents are showing middle-aged couples around the grounds. The place looks like a mini manor estate. A fountain has been installed in the courtyard. They've mowed the field and started building another new house.

Weekend. S. and I go to Norwich to see some of her old university friends. I suggest a pub, but her friends don't like pubs, S. tells me, especially not the ones I like. Old man pubs, they call my haunts. We meet them in one of the new coffee bars and immediately they start talking while they look things up on their phones and show them to each other. They're all around ten years younger than me. I can't follow their rapid-fire conversation. By the time I've thought about a reply to something one of them has brought up, they're onto a second or third topic. It's like being in a real-life social media app. I try to keep up but eventually tune out and go outside to smoke. There's an estate agent's opposite that used to be a rough pub, one of the first I went to when I arrived in Norwich, before it became gentrified. I remember filling in a university form there and being asked for money by a guy with a dog on a rope. As I go back inside, it strikes me for the first time that I'm approaching middle age. Strange feeling.

Time has been harnessed and sped up. We're pulled along, almost ahead of ourselves, or left behind. The corporate colonisation of the world is an assault not only on nature but also on time. It captures us in its own time, which is no time at all, but a constant deferral. It exploits the present for profit. We're sold the latest innovation, the thing that matters most this instant, only to be shown something that matters even more the next. We're told it's in our interest to expose our private lives to businesses because it'll save us time, give us immediate access to whatever we want. Isn't part of the reason for the success of social media that it holds out a false moment to us and uses our desire to grasp for it? The more impatiently we reach for it, the further the moment withdraws; it's always bigger than us. How better to profit from it than to create a parody of meaningful time that appeals to our basest desires?

On the stock markets, whose movements have effects that ripple across the globe and shape our lives, even out here in Broadland, high-frequency trading is approaching the speed of light. Advanced communication networks using algorithms, microwave towers, and lasers now enable traders seeking an edge to make more than a hundred thousand transactions per second. On barren industrial estates, companies compete to move closer to dishes and data centres so they can boost the speed of their trades by milliseconds. That's the current landscape, serious people say. That's just how the economy works these days.

I watch a fight between a couple of territorial blackbirds on the lawn. The winner leaves his rival stunned on the ground. I consider going out to check on it, but after a while the defeated bird starts flapping again and flies off to find another patch.

We've been lazy about gardening. The weeds are already getting out of hand, but the daffodils are just as tall, and on calm days they turn slowly, almost imperceptibly, to follow the sun from dawn to dusk.

Emerson:

> Our life is an apprenticeship to the truth that around every circle another can be drawn; that there is no end in nature, but every end is a beginning; that there is always another dawn risen on mid-noon, and under every deep a lower deep opens.

If the instant is a shrinking circle, the moment is an expanding one. It holds the past and future within it, and it's in its nature to grow and take you with it as far as your mind can bear—until you turn away in boredom or fear, shift your attention to something else, come up with clever reasons to forget about it.

The moment lurks inside everyday time; always new, always the same. It waits to give you back your life, like an event long prepared without your knowledge, like an act of fate. It *needs* you: your ragged past, your timid present, your whirl of thoughts, your hoard of words. It waits for you to step into the light of day, where it can find you and let you come into your own.

Some days it seems as if the things I type here have been formulating themselves for years, in the sleep of my life, as Duras said, so that in a sense I'm only taking minutes on some ongoing proceeding. Other days, it's as if I'm describing things for the first time.

The days are getting longer. I've felt a sense of peace lately, the kind of composure I imagined I'd grow into when I was younger and had no control over my life. I used to picture my future self looking back at his agitated past and cringing. What was being young but an endless wait to get older and wiser? I was naïve and knew it, because I was so often reminded of it by my elders. I wanted to get older so I too could benefit from hard-won experience. I suspected that these feelings were themselves experiences I might benefit from, but resented the humiliations of youth, of having to live through a series of scary tests that only the older self can resolve. Now, having grown into my future self, I look back with mixed feelings. Relief, but also things I never imagined, slightly frightening: awareness of the ageing body, that your time on earth will come to an end, and that you may even come to feel it was too short.

I've gotten rid of my smartphone and bought an old-fashioned dumbphone, like the ones we used to use in the nineties. It can only text and make calls. Texting takes much longer, so I only do it when I need to. I'll lose work and disappoint some project managers—I've already lost work—but so be it.

A slow, beautiful evening. Rose and lilac sky over Kirkwood, perfectly indifferent. Light that brings me back to the Danish coast of my childhood. After a drizzle the garden gleams and the birds sing loudly—joyfully, it seems to me, at least at this moment. I call S. over and we stand at the window with Rookie as the sky gently overwhelms us. Then I remember I have a deadline in the morning and go back to my laptop.

Publisher's Note

The following is a list of the sources quoted throughout *The Moment*, preceded by the numbers of the pages on which they appear. Sources without a named publisher are available in the public domain.

4:     E.M. Cioran, *The Trouble With Being Born*, 1973. Translated by Richard Howard, published by Simon and Schuster, 2013.

5:     André Gide, *The Counterfeiters*, 1925. Translated by Dorothy Bussy, published by Knopf, 1951.

15:    Virginia Woolf, *To the Lighthouse*, 1927.

19:    Franz Kafka, *The Diaries: 1910–1923*. Published by Schocken, 1976. 1910–1913, translated by Joseph Kresh; 1914–1923, translated by Martin Greenberg with the co-operation of Hannah Arendt.

19:    Samuel Beckett, *The Unnamable*, 1953. Published by Faber, 2010.

20:    Maurice Blanchot, *The Space of Literature*, 1955. Original translation by Peter Holm Jensen, 2020.

24:    Karl Jaspers, *The Psychology of Worldviews*, 1919. Translated by Françoise Balibar, Philippe Büttgen, and Barbara Cassin, in *Dictionary of Untranslatables: A Philosophical Lexicon*, published by Princeton University Press, 2014.

36:    John Berger, 'Why Look at Animals?' in *About Looking*. Published by Bloomsbury, 1980.

41:    Rainer Maria Rilke, 'The Eighth Elegy' from *The Duino Elegies*, 1922. Original translation by Jenny Reddish, 2020.

44:    Virginia Woolf, 'A Sketch of the Past', 1939.

55:    Ralph Waldo Emerson, 'Circles', 1841.

59:    Mark Fisher, *Capitalist Realism: Is There No Alternative?* Published by Zero Books, 2009.

60:    Gerard Manley Hopkins, 'God's Grandeur', 1877.

65:    Gerard Manley Hopkins, 'God's Grandeur', 1877.

77:    Mark Fisher, *Capitalist Realism: Is There No Alternative?* Published by Zero Books, 2009.

108:        Rainer Maria Rilke, *Letters to a Young Poet*, 1929. Original translation by Peter Holm Jensen, 2020.

116:        Sean Parker quoted in Olivia Solon, 'Ex-Facebook president Sean Parker: site made to exploit human 'vulnerability''. Published in *The Guardian*, 9 November 2017: <theguardian.com/technology/ 2017/nov/09/facebook-sean-parker-vulnerability-brain-psychology>

125:        Blaise Pascal, *Pensées*, 1670. Translated by A.J. Krailsheimer, published by Penguin, 1966, revised 1995.

136:        Martin Heidegger, *Nietzsche*, 1966. Translated by David Farrell Krell, published by HarperCollins, 1991.

136:        Mark Cocker, *Claxton: Field Notes from a Small Planet*. Published by Jonathan Cape, 2014.

147:        Witold Gombrowicz, *Diary*, 1969. Translated by Lillian Vallee, published by Yale University Press, 2012.

149–150:   Rainer Maria Rilke, from a letter written in 1915. Original translation by Peter Holm Jensen, 2020.

150:        Rainer Maria Rilke, poem from a letter written in 1914. Original translation by Peter Holm Jensen, 2020.

151:        Rainer Maria Rilke, 'The Second Elegy' from *The Duino Elegies*, 1922. Original translation by Peter Holm Jensen, 2020.

155:        W.S. Graham, 'Notes on a Poetry of Release', 1946.

161:        Wallace Stevens, 'The Well Dressed Man With a Beard' in *Parts of a World*, published by Knopf, 1942.

163–167:   Franz Kafka, *The Blue Octavo Notebooks*, 1948. Edited by Max Brod, translated by Ernst Kaiser and Eithne Wilkins, published by Exact Change, 1991.

164:        Franz Kafka, *The Zurau Aphorisms*, 1931. "Hold the world's coat" translated by Michael Hofmann, published by Random House, 2006.

165:        Richie Robertson, *Kafka: A Very Short Introduction*, published by Oxford University Press, 2004.

167:        Roberto Calasso, afterword to *The Zurau Aphorisms* translated by Michael Hoffman, published by Random House, 2006.

169:        Franz Kafka, *Letters to Felice*, 1967. Translated by James Stern and Elizabeth Duckworth, published by Schocken, 1973.

169-170:   Rainer Maria Rilke, from a letter written in 1921. Original translation by Peter Holm Jensen, 2020.

175:        Martin Heidegger, 'Why Poets?', 1946, in *Heidegger: Off the Beaten Track*, 1950. Edited and translated by Julian Young and Kenneth Haynes, published by Cambridge University Press, 2002.

179:        Meister Eckhart, translator unknown.

183:        William S. Burroughs, *Junkie*. Published by Ace Books, 1953.

184:        Gaston Bachelard, 'Poetic Instant and Metaphysical Instant', 1939, in *Intuition of the Instant*. Translated by Eileen Rizo-Patron, published by Northwestern University Press, 2013.

184–185:   Maurice Merleau-Ponty, *Phenomenology of Perception*, 1945. Translated by Colin Smith, published by Routledge, 1958.

186:        Rainer Maria Rilke, from a letter written in 1920. Original translation by Peter Holm Jensen, 2020.

194:        William S. Burroughs, *Letters, Volume 1*. Edited by Oliver Harris, published by Penguin, 1993.

198:        Martin Heidegger, 'Dialogue Between a Japanese and an Enquirer' in *On the Way to Language*, 1959. Translated by Peter D. Hertz, published by Harper, 1971.

205:        Søren Kierkegaard, *The Concept of Anxiety*, 1844. Edited and translated by Reidar Thomte, published by Princeton University Press, 1981.

206:        Søren Kierkegaard, *Philosophical Fragments, or a Fragment of Philosophy*, 1844. Edited and translated by Edna H. Hong and Howard V. Hong, published by Princeton University Press, 1985.

215:        Maurice Blanchot, *Thomas the Obscure*, 1976. Translated by Robert Lamberton, published by Station Hill Press, 1988.

215:        Michel Haar, 'Empty Time and Indifference to Being' in *Heidegger Toward the Turn: Essays on the Work of the 1930s*. Edited by James Risser, published by SUNY Press, 1999.

228:        Charles E. Scott, *Living With Indifference*, published by Indiana University Press, 2007.

233:        Ralph Waldo Emerson, 'Circles', 1841.

Image Credits

Prefatory: Double-page spread from *The Land of the Broads* (1885) by Ernest Richard Suffling. Digitised by the British Library on Flickr without copyright restrictions.

13: St. Andrew's Church, Kirby Bedon, Norfolk. Photograph by David (brokentaco) on Flickr, converted into monochrome, used under Creative Commons license CC BY 2.0.

40: Strumpshaw Fen, Norfolk. Photograph by Michael Button (michaeljohnbutton) on Flickr, cropped and converted into monochrome, used under Creative Commons license CC BY 2.0.

85: Blakeney Point, Norfolk. Photograph by Brian Toward (histogram_man) on Flickr, converted into monochrome, used under Creative Commons license CC0 1.0.

196: Gammel Lejre skibssætning, Denmark. Photograph by user Lichterfelder on Wikimedia Commons, cropped and converted into monochrome, used under Creative Commons license CC BY 3.0.

SPLICE

ThisIsSplice.co.uk

Lightning Source UK Ltd.
Milton Keynes UK
UKHW040907140221
378640UK00001BA/15/J